Little Gems

Onyx

2017

ROMANCE WRITERS *of Australia*

Onyx 2017: Little Gems Anthology

Anthology of Short Stories published by
Romance Writers of Australia Inc
© 2017

Ebook format: 978-0-9577361-1-5
Print format: 978-0-9577361-0-8
Little Gems Coordinator: Lis Hoorweg
Cover design by Lana Pecherczyk
Edited by Laura Greaves
Proofread by Claire Boston

Little Gems

Onyx

Short Story Anthology
2017

Other Little Gems Anthologies

Foreword

This year our Little Gems central gem is Onyx – and what a perfect gem that is to use as inspiration for a story of romance and hope.

When I looked into the history of the Onyx, I discovered that it is a gem found across the world. It has been used in mundane items such as bowls and plates, to being used to create magnificent pieces of sculpture, jewellery and distinctive cameos. It is even used as a distinctive and beautiful architectural feature. Onyx could be called a truly universal gem.

But that isn't all. A variant of Onyx, called Sardonyx, was believed by ancient Roman soldiers to bestow courage. They would carve a depiction of Mars, the God of War, onto the surface and carry the talisman into battle. Ancient English midwives would place Sardonyx between the breasts of labouring women to ease childbirth. In Renaissance Europe, carrying a piece of Onyx was thought to bestow eloquence. Persians hold a traditional belief that it helps with epilepsy – so it is a stone of hope.

Courage. Hope. Relief from trials and pain. Eloquence. Used in everyday life, but also to bring beauty and express creativity. The more I read, the more I realised Onyx is a stone that represents romance writers and the romance genre at its core, for at our core, we must be as hard as Onyx to persevere, but like Onyx, we are an instrument to express beauty and hope. A truly perfect gem to be the symbol of romance writers and the romance genre.

It is with great pleasure, that in my last year as President of RWA, I am given the privilege of bringing this Little Gems:

Onyx Anthology to you all. I congratulate all the authors who won a place in this anthology – brilliant work all of you.

And to the reader, I hope that in these stories, you will find that the writers have carved out a treasure of romantic hope and beauty in the true spirit of this remarkable gem.

Leisl Leighton
RWA President 2014-2017

Onyx Magic
By
Heidi Catherine

The day Rachel got married was the second best day of her life. The day she got divorced was the best.

Marrying Thomas had been a mistake of catastrophic proportions. Not that she'd known that on her wedding day. She'd been so happy she thought she was going to burst. But when her divorce came through she actually had burst ... into huge tears of relief that left her eyes red for a week.

Now when she looked at her wedding photos she wanted to shout at her younger self to run, far away and fast. But of course the girl with the long veil couldn't hear her, destined to walk down that aisle towards a man who told more lies than she had beads on her dress.

Rachel swept her dark hair into a ponytail and tucked her house key into her sock. A run would do her good. Her sister had been nagging her to exercise more regularly. And unless you counted drinking coffee as exercise then Rachel wasn't really doing it very regularly at all. Not that Emma needed to know that. She might be a personal trainer, but she was still her little sister, even if they were in their thirties now.

She headed down the end of her street, keeping up a gentle but steady jog that she hoped she could maintain for at least a few blocks.

'Excuse me,' a deep voice called from the other side of the road.

She slowed her pace and turned to see a man holding a lead minus one very important thing—a dog.

'Have you seen a little black dog?' he asked, crossing the road to speak to her.

'No, I've only just set out,' she said, coming to a stop. Perhaps the universe was telling her exercise wasn't so important after all.

The man ran his hand through his thick blond hair and let out a sigh. Rachel's stomach lurched to see him in such distress. He looked so strong and capable, not the sort to fall to pieces over a lost pet.

She'd always wanted a dog, but Thomas wouldn't hear of it. He thought they made too much mess. How ironic that Thomas himself had been the one to make such a mess of things that both their lives fell apart. Although looking at this man she thought perhaps not having a dog was better than going through the pain of losing one. Not all that dissimilar to her marriage really.

'No worries, thanks anyway,' the man said.

'I'll keep an eye out for him.' Rachel wished she could do more. He seemed like a nice guy and it was sweet to imagine someone so tall and well built was owner of a little black dog. He must attract all sorts of girls walking around with a chick magnet like that. Or maybe it was his girlfriend's dog and he was trying to get it back for her. Guys as attractive as him were never single. What a shame! She could just about break her 'man ban' for someone like him.

He flashed Rachel a quick smile that failed to reach his grey eyes and hurried away, leaving her imagining what his smile would be like if it were genuine. Undoubtedly it would make him even more gorgeous.

She picked up her jog again and turned the corner at the end of the street, ignoring her lungs screaming for oxygen for another block before slowing to a fast walk. Emma was right. She needed to exercise. Not for her weight—she lost enough of that after the break up—but for her head. She could feel her negative thoughts clearing already. Perhaps nagging little sisters did know something after all.

A car screeched to a halt ahead of her and she saw a small shadow dart out onto the footpath. The dog!

The car took off again and Rachel found a surprise reserve

of energy and ran over to the dog, who was sniffing a fence post, oblivious to how close he'd come to death.

He looked like one of those designer 'oodle' types of dog, a mixed breed of cute and crazy. Definitely a chick magnet.

'Hello,' she said, bobbing down and slipping a finger under his collar. 'I've got you now.'

The dog wriggled to get free, but Rachel scooped him up and held him firmly. He relaxed in her arms, seeming to accept that his quest for freedom was over.

'Good boy,' she soothed, turning his collar so she could read the tag. There was a phone number underneath some cursive script with the dog's name.

'Onyx,' she said out loud. The dog's ears pricked up in response. 'That's a very posh name.'

Dangling from the collar next to the tag was a small pendant set with a dark stone, prompting Rachel's memory that an onyx was a gemstone.

'Well, you *are* a posh dog.' She laughed. 'You're wearing nicer jewellery than me.'

She turned back towards home so she could call the number on the tag. Hopefully she'd run into the owner again on her way back.

Despite being a small dog, Onyx soon got heavy, but she dared not put him down in case he made another dash for freedom. His owner would be so happy when she returned him safely. She pictured him flashing her that gorgeous genuine smile she'd imagined as he held out a bunch of thank you flowers. Not that she expected flowers, of course. It was just that it'd been a long time since she'd received any. Thomas didn't see the sense in spending money on something that was already dying before you even bought it.

She put her key in the front door and decided she really needed to stop thinking about Thomas. It was over. It'd been over since the moment she'd found that message from Lisa on his phone. It'd probably been over long before that, only she hadn't known it.

Setting Onyx down on her kitchen floor, she found a plastic container and filled it with water. He lapped it up enthusiastically, then turned to grin at her. Did dogs grin? He certainly seemed to.

'Come here,' she said, patting his thick, dark fur. He really did have the sweetest little face with those big eyes and floppy ears.

She looked at the phone number on his tag again, only to discover one of the middle digits had completely rubbed away. Finding his owner may not be as easy as she'd thought. But still, not impossible. She was just going to have to make ten calls instead of one.

She started by inserting the number one into the blank space and dialling. A woman answered. Handsome man's girlfriend perhaps? No, she wasn't missing a dog thank you very much. The woman huffed and hung up before Rachel even had the chance to apologise for bothering her.

On her second attempt she got the voicemail for a man who sounded far older than the one she'd met on the street. She left a message anyway and moved onto number three. With any luck this would be the one.

By the time she got to number nine, she realised luck wasn't on her side. She'd had to leave three messages in total. None of them sounded like Onyx's owner. It was strange he wasn't answering his phone. He'd seemed pretty desperate. She'd have thought he'd be carrying his phone everywhere.

'Let's get you something to eat,' said Rachel, fossicking about for some leftovers.

Onyx wagged his tail at the bowl full of food she set down in front of him and tucked in.

'Slow down!' Rachel shook her head, laughing.

Her phone buzzed from the kitchen table and her laughter dried up.

'That will be your owner,' she said as Onyx licked the bottom of the bowl.

But it wasn't. It was Emma.

'Hey sis, how are you?'

'Onyx! Stop it! Hang on, Em … '

Onyx had pushed the empty bowl towards the water bowl and was about to topple it over. She picked him up and carried him to her backyard, sitting down on the grass with him.

'Sorry, Em. You there?'

'Who's Onyx? Tell me everything.'

'Don't get too excited,' said Rachel, hearing the excitement in her sister's voice. 'He's a dog.'

'Oh. You didn't tell me you bought a dog.' Emma's voice dropped to an offended tone.

'I found him and now I'm trying to find his owner.'

'Why don't you take him to the pound to see if he's microchipped?'

'He's got a number on his tag. I'm just waiting for a call back.' Rachel plucked a blade of grass from the lawn and Onyx bounded over and sniffed at her hand.

'You sound distracted. Why don't you call me later, once you've knocked off from the dog rescue centre?'

'He's really cute, Em.'

'Maybe his owner will be, too.'

Rachel sighed. 'He is.'

'What? You've met him?'

'I'll explain later.' The phone beeped with another call coming through. 'I gotta go.'

A man was on the other line, calling back to say it wasn't his dog. She crossed his number off his list and thanked him for returning her call.

That left two more calls to wait for.

When the day stretched into evening, she started to wonder if Emma was right. Maybe she should take Onyx to the pound to check for a microchip.

Deciding to wait until the morning, she made Onyx a bed from an old jumper, which he immediately rejected in favour of jumping on her bed and curling up next to her.

'Does your owner let you sleep on his bed?' she asked, shaking her head.

Onyx closed his eyes and drifted off to sleep as if this were the most normal thing in the world.

'I guess he does,' said Rachel, running her fingers over the smooth pendant dangling from his collar.

Why would anyone put such a pendant on a dog? She reached for her phone and typed the word *onyx* into a search engine.

There was a lot of technical geological information, but one sentence jumped out at her almost immediately.

An onyx defends against negativity, helping to release sadness while assisting with letting go of unhappy relationships.

She couldn't deny that ever since she'd found Onyx she felt exactly like that. Or was it since she met his owner? The pain at her separation from Thomas felt different somehow. He was more like someone who'd hurt her in the past than someone with the power to hurt her now. Perhaps this stone did have some kind of magical powers.

Onyx groaned in his sleep and lifted his head to rest it on her arm.

Or perhaps it wasn't the stone at all. This dog was a very special kind of dog. So why hadn't his owner returned her call?

Rachel slept more soundly than she had in months, grateful it was the weekend so she could lie in. Sunday mornings were her favourite time of the week, even better than Fridays when she shut down her computer at her accounting firm. Sunday mornings were about drinking coffee and reading the paper or maybe pottering in her garden.

But perhaps not this Sunday morning, she thought as she woke to Onyx licking her chin.

'Stop that,' she said, putting her pillow over her face.

Onyx seemed to think this was a great game, trying to burrow under the pillow to get to her.

'Okay, you win,' she said, dragging herself out of bed and heading down the hallway. She'd have her coffee outside today so Onyx could explore. Then maybe she'd try those two phone numbers again.

Little footsteps followed her and she opened the back door, glad to see the sun shining.

Onyx dashed past and lifted his leg on the silver birch on her lawn.

She left him while she made her coffee, then settled down at her outdoor setting to watch Onyx perform a close inspection of her newly planted veggie patch.

'Don't you dare eat my tomatoes,' she said, lifting her mug to take a sip. The coffee had spilled over and left a perfect 'O' shape on the table. She ran her finger through the liquid, watching the way it seeped into the timber.

There was something about the O that nagged at her, causing her to splutter on her coffee when she realised what it was.

O, or more specifically, zero. Zero! She'd started at number one yesterday looking for Onyx's owner and finished with number nine, without trying zero. And to think she was an accountant. She wouldn't be telling her colleagues about this one.

She left Onyx once more to get her phone from beside her bed and tried the number, this time inserting the all-important zero.

'Hello, Liam speaking,' said a voice she immediately knew was the right one. Liam. That suited him.

'Hi, this is Rachel. I met you yesterday when you were looking for your dog.'

'You've found him? Oh my god, please tell me you've found him.'

Rachel laughed. The excitement in his voice was infectious, making her stomach lurch in an entirely different way to how he had the day before.

'Yes. I'm so sorry. I found him yesterday, but your number isn't clear on his tag. I had a bit of trouble tracking you down.'

'Oh, thank god. I've been meaning to replace that tag. Thank you. I haven't slept a wink. I thought he was gone forever. Where did you find him?'

'A couple of blocks from where I met you, down on Johnson Street.'

'Were you the blonde lady with the pram or the cute one with dark hair who doesn't know how to jog?'

'I do so know how to jog!' Her face flushed, not at the jogging comment, but at being called cute by a guy who personified that very word himself.

'Only teasing. Sorry, I'm just excited. Can I come and pick him up?'

'Of course.' Hopefully her cheeks would have calmed down by then or he might mistake her for one of the tomatoes in her veggie patch.

She gave him her address and raced inside to change out of her pyjamas. Onyx followed, sensing something interesting was happening. She really did need to get a dog. It was nice having company like this. Maybe she'd make a visit to the pound after all. She'd see if Emma wanted to come with her. Or maybe not. She'd probably make her adopt a greyhound to really keep her fit. A nice little dog like Onyx would be far more appropriate.

She pulled on some jeans and a t-shirt and quickly brushed her hair and teeth, pausing only for a brief few seconds to try to figure out what Liam had seen when he'd referred to her as cute. She had to admit he was right about one thing. She definitely didn't know how to jog.

Her doorbell rang and Onyx sped to the front door, turning in circles and barking.

Rachel felt a little bit the same. It wasn't every day that a man as gorgeous as Liam knocked on her door, even if he was there for a dog instead of her.

She opened it and watched Liam crouch down to fuss over a very excited Onyx.

Liam looked up at her and she noticed his eyes were dark blue, not grey, complementing the fair tone of his skin. He smiled.

Yep. There it was. That genuine smile, even more gorgeous than she'd imagined.

'Thank you so much for keeping him safe,' he said, trying to get Onyx to calm down.

'My pleasure. He's beautiful. I've got to ask you though … why did you call him Onyx?'

'He was a gift from my mum,' he said, wincing as Onyx landed a sloppy kiss on his lips. 'She gave him to me just before she died. She was into crystals and stuff and said he'd help me heal.'

'Has he?' Rachel bit her tongue for asking such a personal question.

Liam stood, leaving Onyx to sniff at an apparently fascinating pot plant.

'He has actually. I reckon he's got magical properties.'

As if on cue, Onyx lifted his leg on the pot.

'You watch,' said Liam. 'That plant will sprout roses by the end of the day.'

Rachel laughed. 'You know, I wouldn't be surprised.'

'Which reminds me,' said Liam, running back to his car, which he'd parked in her driveway. He reached for something on the front seat and returned with a pink rose that looked to have been hurriedly plucked from a garden. 'I pinched this from my neighbour on my way out. It's for you, for taking care of Onyx.'

Rachel took the flower and held it to her nose. It wasn't quite the bunch of flowers she'd imagined, but coming from Liam it was even better.

'Thank you, but really, I think he was the one who took care of me,' she said.

'I'm going to take him for that walk he missed out on when he got away from me yesterday.' He hesitated, and ran his fingers through his hair like he had when she first met him. 'Would you like to come with us?'

A shot of excitement sparked up Rachel's spine. 'As long as there's no jogging involved then count me in.'

Liam's laugh was deep and husky, making his eyes twinkle as that painfully attractive smile lit up his face.

That website about the onyx seemed to have known what it was talking about, except it left something out. Onyx wasn't just good at helping to let go of relationships, it seemed it might also be good at bringing about new ones.

Yes, Liam was right. Onyx most definitely had magical properties.

Return to Mingardi
By
Fiona Greene

The highway no longer passed through Mingardi.

Neither did the traffic, if Main Street was anything to go by. Nina Bartholemew slowed her car to a crawl as she passed Sinclairs. Her teenage utopia was still trading, even if its famous façade was peeling. She rolled down the window and sniffed.

The umbrellas standing guard over the diner's picnic tables were a far cry from the firetruck red of her memories, but the aroma of hot barbecued beef was the same.

Delicious.

Sinful.

She cruised the deserted strip, revisiting memories of hot summer nights and boys in fast cars. 'See,' she told herself as she pulled up at the T-junction on the other side of town, 'It's not so bad.' She flicked her indicator on and, as she did so, caught sight of 'the tree'.

Skinny and underfed, the gum had sprouted on top of a massive stump, a single seed catching in a rough spot on the sawn edge. Unable to push its roots down, it did the next best thing and sent roots out and over the stump, finally finding earth.

It was a thing of legend around town; part meeting place, part navigation marker. To Nina it symbolised the struggle.

The struggle of life in Mingardi.

Now her dad, the last remaining family member in town, was gone.

The indicator ticked in the silence. She flicked it off as she stared at the tree's leaves dancing in the breeze.

'Damn.' She wasn't ready for this. Stomach churning, Nina executed a U-turn and sped back the way she'd come, only slowing as she drove back into town. 'Double Damn.' She parked in front of Sinclairs.

No one knew she was here. They weren't expecting her today. If she left now, she could disappear back to the city.

The zero-fuss option.

No.

The last time she'd spoken to her father, she'd promised to finalise everything out at the family property.

Nina sucked in a shuddery breath.

She'd keep that promise, but only when *she* was ready.

~ * ~

The bell tinkled overhead as Nina pushed the heavy wooden door and stepped into the warmth of Sinclairs. A brisk walk around town had left her more conflicted than ever. Shops, empty and marked 'for lease', far outnumbered the businesses that remained.

'Hi. You're fine to take a seat. I'll come and get your order in a sec.'

The rich baritone dragged Nina out of her funk. She glanced up, and the air was sucked out of her lungs. 'Max?'

Max Fairchild.

God help me.

'Yep.' His smile was instant then the menu tucked under his arm hit the floor with a thud. 'Nina?'

They stared at each other for a full ten seconds before Nina said, 'In the flesh.'

Max scooped up the menu. As he stood, his eyes raked her body. 'I remember.'

Nina's cheeks heated. 'Turns out there are some things that haven't changed in Mingardi.'

Run. Run now.

'A few,' Max confirmed.

Nina peeled off her coat, surveying the deserted diner. 'Where is everybody?'

'Onyx is more of a lunch/dinner venue than a cafe now.'

'Onyx?' Nina glanced around and noted the updated décor, natural timber highlighted with silver and black. 'Did you sell the farm?'

Max smiled again and Nina's knees buckled. 'Nope. We've rebranded. We figured out what the market wants and now instead of running Fairchild Pastoral, we're Onyx Cattle Company, the district's biggest supplier of Black Angus beef to the Asian market. Onyx showcases our beef.'

'Wow.' Nina blinked then looked around. 'Wow.'

'We're open for the locals, tourists, and the occasional function, but there's more money in trade delegations and, as funny as it sounds, catering for Chinese golfing tours.' His face lit up when he talked about the restaurant, then his smile faded. 'It's the way of it now.'

Nina nodded. 'No more Saturday nights around the jukebox, followed by early morning bacon and egg recovery sessions.'

Their eyes met and Nina held Max's gaze for an eternity. His eyes darkened at the shared memory. 'I'd forgotten about that. We still do a bit of morning stuff—a coffee cart for the farmer's market—but it's all changed since the last time you were in town.'

'I'll say.' Nina was having trouble getting her head around bad boy Max Fairchild running a restaurant. The last time she'd seen him he'd been heading for the US rodeo circuit with his boots, a backpack and a bucket full of bravado.

And she'd been here, facing the music.

This Max, with his close-cropped hair and strong, wiry body intrigued her. 'How'd you end up here? What happened?'

'To the Sinclairs?'

Nina rolled her eyes. That wasn't what she meant and he knew it.

He eyed her curiously. 'You're really interested?'

'I am,' she said softly. 'I left town; I didn't chop up all my memories and start a bonfire.'

'That's not what I heard.'

Nina's eyes prickled with unshed tears. Of all people, she'd thought Max might have understood.

She was wrong.

Hands shaking, she gathered up her coat.

'Stop.' He put a hand on her arm. 'I'm sorry. I'm the last person who should have an opinion here.'

'Damn right, Mr I'm-Going-To-Make-It-Big-In-The-States'.

Max lifted his shirt and turned. 'Fourteen fractured vertebrae. Two titanium rods. I could have kept riding but I kinda got sick of explaining myself in airport security.'

Nina groped behind her for a chair, a table, anything. His back, once smooth and tanned and perfect for running your fingers over, was a patchwork of scars. 'Mighty big cuts.' Somehow she stayed upright.

'My ex didn't like the look of them either. I suggested she take her sensitive eyeballs and find something else to look at.' Max grimaced. 'But I've seen worse. At least I'm still walking.'

Another wave of dizziness hit and she sank down into the booth behind her.

'Hey.' Max crossed the space between them in seconds. 'You okay?' He squatted down and put his hands on her shoulders to steady her. His fingertips burned through her lightweight shirt.

Nina took a huge gulp of air. 'I'm good.'

'Great, because picking you up off the floor would be bad for business. And for my back.' He laughed then made a show of bending and twisting. 'It's okay now. So long as I don't limbo, that is.'

Nina tried to smile at the joke and failed. 'How it is even possible for you to have been injured so badly, yet nothing came across my radar?'

'You know small towns. Full of secrets and lies and past feuds. Your dad made it clear that he didn't want you to know.'

Nina felt the familiar burn, deep in her chest, 'And yet my falls from grace were fodder for the entire community. I'm pretty sure I could feel the curtains twitching down Main Street as I drove through.'

Max's face hardened. 'You know it wasn't your fault, right? Everyone that was there that night had a part in what happened. We all have to shoulder some responsibility. It wasn't down to you.'

Nina's hands started to sweat. 'I was driving.'

'We'd all had a turn driving. We're lucky more people

weren't hurt.'

'I'm pretty sure Dad didn't care about other people; he was only interested in the Bartholemew heir.'

Max stiffened. 'Grant?'

'Of course Grant,' Nina confirmed. 'What else ...' She stopped and traced the grain of the tabletop. Then she swallowed. Losing her brother in the accident had been horrific, but there'd been more.

Max slid into the booth and took hold of her hand. 'I'm sorry for talking about Grant. Especially now. That was insensitive.' He paused. 'I was sorry to hear about your dad. He was a good man. Even though he never said it, I know he cared for you.'

Nina's breath hitched. Tears prickled and she blinked to hold them back. 'Thank you.' She tilted her head. This was the man her father had considered unacceptable for his only daughter. When she'd first arrived, she'd thought the successful businessman was a veneer, thickly layered over Max's inner larrikin.

Now she wasn't so sure.

A weight descended on her shoulders as she realised just how wrong her father had been about Max. If the papers in her bag were any indication, Max wasn't the only thing he'd misjudged.

Don't think about that now.

She pasted a smile on her face and changed the subject. 'Have you still got Thunder?' Growing up, the stockhorse had been Max's pride and joy.

'Yeah, he's older, greyer. He's retired from riding, but we still bond over an apple most days.'

Thunder had been majestic in his prime. The thought of his weary bones confined to a paddock made her heart ache.

'I've got a couple of horses, direct descendants. Maybe we could go riding?'

Nina damped down on the thrill Max's offer gave her. 'I don't know.' How much should she tell him? 'Dad's had some trouble out on the farm. I'm not sure how long I'll be in town.'

Max nodded and laid his hand over hers. 'It's a hard life out here. Too much can go wrong. We were lucky. Right place, right time to capitalise.' He squeezed her fingers. 'Others weren't so fortunate.'

He knew.

Her breath escaped in a whoosh. 'You're right.'

The warmth of his fingers resting over hers lifted the weight from her shoulders. Maybe if she talked to Max?

She fumbled around in her bag for the legal papers as the bell over the door jangled.

'Delivery.' An older woman in a high-vis vest pushed through into the café.

'Be right there.' Max's look was long and smouldering, then he pushed to his feet. 'Sorry, duty calls.'

Nina's hand stilled in her bag. What was she thinking? Max was her past, not her future. 'I should go.'

Max had started walking but he stopped, wrote something on his order pad. 'Here's my number. We open tonight till eight and I'll be free after the last customer's main is plated. We could catch up over the best Black Angus in Australia if you're interested?' He handed her the folded slip. 'Call me, let me know what you decide.'

'I'll see.' Nina kept her answer deliberately vague. She tucked the number into her bag and watched him charm the delivery driver, who smiled and laughed and played with her hair.

Nina knew exactly how she felt.

As she rugged up to venture back into the cold, she watched the man she'd thought she'd grow old with and sighed.

Returning to Mingardi was harder than she'd ever imagined.

~ * ~

Nina had changed her mind a thousand times and her accessories at least six, but come eight o'clock she was right where the universe was telling her she should be. At the booth in Onyx where they'd spoken this morning.

The waitress had already delivered a basket of bread and a glass of red. Nina sipped the wine as snippets of conversations about cattle prices, teaching methods and television shows floated past.

Onyx certainly attracted a diverse crowd.

Seconds after eight o'clock, Max appeared and slid into the

booth beside her.

Nina gestured to the table. 'I'm pretty sure this is set for you to sit over there.'

Max settled himself more comfortably, the heat from his thigh radiating onto hers. 'So I'm a rule breaker.' He shifted so his thigh was touching. 'I'm pretty sure that's what you liked about me.' Heat flooded her body. She took a long sip of her wine to stop herself from grabbing the menu and fanning. Or from grabbing Max.

'You *are* a rule breaker.' She gestured to the tables filled with customers. 'Remember school, when the girls couldn't do shop classes and the boys weren't allowed near the cooking lessons? What the hell happened?'

'Barbecue school.'

Nina choked on her wine. 'Barbecue school?' Of all the things she'd expected him to say, barbecue school was not one of them.

'One of the US grill manufacturers sponsored me. Weekends I did rodeo. Weekdays I did cooking demos. In chaps. But first I had to go to barbecue school.'

Chaps.

Nina's mouth went dry. 'Shirtless in chaps?'

Max had the good grace to look sheepish. 'It was a very good deal. A motorhome and everything.'

Nina took another gulp of wine. 'Stetson?'

Max raised a brow. 'Seriously?' Then he added, 'Akubra.'

Her wine glass was empty. 'Waxed?'

He nodded. 'And oiled.'

She reached for the water.

'I'm not sure what was more dangerous. Riding the bulls in the arena or half-naked cooking over an open grill with my chest slathered in baby oil.'

Nina's water glass hit the table with a thud.

She couldn't speak.

Couldn't breathe.

He might not have caught fire, but there a real possibility she was going to. 'If I Google that, are there photos?'

He nodded. 'Cooking Cowboys Rodeo Team.'

'You're serious, aren't you? All of this,' she gestured around the restaurant, 'because of that?'

'Indirectly.' Max was saved from any further questions by the arrival of their waitress.

Nina's mouth watered as their meals were served. The presentation wasn't fancy; a prime sirloin, grilled to perfection, served with a jacket potato and delicate coleslaw. She sliced off a sliver of beef and popped it into her mouth.

Unlike its rubbery supermarket cousin, this beef was bursting with flavour, tempered with a hint of spice. They ate in silence for a few seconds, then Nina said, 'Spectacular.'

'It's not bad, is it?' Max grinned. 'I can't take all the credit. The Onyx Cattle Company make it easy, all I do is crank up the barbecue.'

This was the Max she remembered. Just being around him made her heart pound. Even though they hadn't spoken for nearly twenty years it was as if they'd never been apart.

Her fantasy of happy ever after screeched to a halt, the succulent beef turning to sawdust.

There was one thing they'd *never* spoken about.

Nina's cutlery clattered onto her plate and she forced herself to chew. And chew. And swallow.

There was probably no future with Max anyway, but she couldn't move forward if they never acknowledged what had happened.

Nina wiped her sweaty palms on her skirt and took a deep breath.

'I …' She couldn't get the words past the lump in her throat. 'I would have told you about the baby.' The words spewed out. 'But I didn't know. Not till they told me at the hospital. After the accident. There was nothing they could do.' When she ran out of words, she squeezed her eyes shut and sank into the backrest.

Max covered her hand with his.

Nina's gaze flicked to his and she choked up at the pain she saw there. She had to look away.

'I'm sorry.' He squeezed her hand gently. 'I'm sorry it happened the way it did and I'm sorry I wasn't there for you. You lost more than anyone that night. Once they patched me up, Dad made sure I left town before it was common knowledge, and like an idiot I shot through. I've regretted it ever since.'

Nina raised her eyes to his. 'You have?'

'Every day.' He slid closer. 'Sometimes, on the circuit, I'd dream about winning it big and coming to find you. Ride in on Thunder and scoop you away from your life to be with me.'

Heat from his thigh burned the length of hers. Instantly she was transported back to the days of shared milkshakes and shared dreams. 'And I would have gone with you.' Her whispered words caught her by surprise, more so when she realised they were true. A spark of anger ignited within her. 'Why didn't you find me?'

Max's thumb moved rhythmically across the back of her hand. 'I wasn't sure you'd have me. I was scared.'

Her anger drained away. Nina reached up and put her finger against his lips, silencing him. 'We both made mistakes. That's in the past.'

Max dropped his gaze to his plate and, after a few seconds, swallowed hard. 'I'm sorry.'

'Me too.'

They sat in silence, each lost in their own thoughts.

Nina sighed. She wasn't here to reconnect with the boy she'd once loved. She'd come as a promise to her father. Yet being with Max, who'd swapped his passion for rodeo for keeping the family farm viable, felt right.

Maybe that inkling she'd had to move back to Mingardi wasn't so stupid after all. She squeezed his hand. 'Enough.' She had to lighten the mood. 'Onyx is awesome and that's because of you. Not because of your shiny, smooth abs or your chaps or the way you turn your steaks. Because of you. That's a huge achievement.'

He didn't answer, just gripped her hand. Eventually he choked out, 'Thank you.'

'You're welcome.' They sat in silence for a few seconds then Nina slid closer so they were fused from shoulder to knee. 'You know this,' she gestured to their plates, 'is too good to let it go cold.' She speared another piece of beef with her fork and put it in her mouth.

After a second, Max nodded and picked up his fork.

Nina chewed then swallowed. 'So this morning we talked about bacon and eggs and recovering together after a hard night.' Heat flooded her cheeks. 'Can you cook anything other than beef?'

Max stared at her for the longest time, then he winked. 'Number one rule of barbecue school—I can't sully the plates here. They're *only* for beef.'

Nina's heart rate skyrocketed. 'But you do have a barbecue at home?'

'Three.' The sheepish grin was back.

'So, hypothetically, if we'd been up all night and needed a bacon and egg recovery session,' the air around them crackled, 'you could probably accommodate that at home?'

Max's eyes darkened and a big grin split his face. He winked again. 'For you, Nina Bartholemew, I'll see what I can do.

Jewels of the Pharaoh
By
Jeff Kenneally

In the pharaoh's own bedroom stood Amunkarnuk and Nemperara. There was no question Amunkarnuk was the brother of the pharaoh. He had the older brother's looks. More importantly, he carried himself as a man only one step from being ruler of the vast empire could. Before him stood the woman he loved. He was four years younger than his brother; Nemperara was four years younger again.

He held her against his chest, his warrior arms wrapping tenderly around her. She leant her head back slightly, allowing her to look him in the eyes.

'What will become of us?' she asked. Her eyes were fearful yet trusting this man would know how to save them. She had the faith of one who knew only love for the man who held her.

They both knew the necklace had been found by the eunuch. Despite his predicament, Amunkarnuk believed this a good thing. Their love could not remain hidden any longer. He could not have let her become another of his brother's wives. The gods had wanted that necklace found. They wanted this. He wanted it.

He gently kissed her lips as he pulled her tightly against him. His hand entwined in her silken hair. These hands, gifted with sword or spear, were as gentle as a nursing mother's as they moved down her back.

In the great hall, Pharaoh Mahunkahme clasped the necklace tightly. His eyes were closed, his face impassive. The backward tilt of his head, the long slow inspiration the only clue of the betrayal searing his heart. Aware the eyes of the eunuch were watching him, he icily steadied himself. He opened his hand and looked at the necklace. The glorious red-banded colour of the onyx stone was beautiful. The ornate gold frame surrounding it made it perfect.

He closed his hand tightly, feeling rage welling.

'Nemperara had this in her possession?' It was a question he already knew the answer to.

'Yes, Pharaoh.'

'Speak of this to nobody.' He looked directly at the eunuch, making him instinctively step backward in fear. 'Nobody,' he added menacingly. He waved his hand once and the eunuch immediately bowed and backed from the great hall.

Mahunkahme slumped into his golden throne, one foot restlessly tapping. He was a man of action with little patience. Twenty-five years of age, he ruled all the Egypt and Palestine lands. His body was brown and muscled. When he smiled, no woman in his kingdom could deny he was truly one of the gods. His dark eyes reflected a sharp intelligence that allowed him to rule this giant empire and its people.

Not all of its people.

He clapped his hands twice, bringing the immediate appearance of his closest aide. High priest Ahmatuk bowed low, his ornate headdress almost falling from his head as he did so. He quickly adjusted his position to keep it steady. The headdress was one of the most ornate in the land, emblazoned with gold and precious stones. Three cobras sprang from the front surrounded by a plumage of ostrich feathers. Amulets spiralled down his arms, more gold and stones.

In contrast, Mahunkahme wore a simple striped neme with its lappets trailing down either side of his face. Subconsciously he ran his hand along the soft silk fabric. Silk was rare and few could trade for it. His neme was perfect quality but in contrast to his priest, he looked like he should be the one bowing.

'Where is my brother?'

Ahmatuk had no idea why he was asked this, nor was it his responsibility to know. He was only almost the most powerful man in the land. The pharaoh's brother was one of two who diminished him.

'I know not, my pharaoh.' He felt nervous without knowing why. Pharaoh was angry and that was trouble enough. Not being able to immediately answer the pharaoh's question put him in harm's way.

'Find him and bring him to me.'

Ahmatuk knew when he was being commanded. He nodded, finding ease in the pharaoh's anger being directed elsewhere. Still, confrontation between brothers could only be bad. He bowed, more careful of his headdress, and hastened from the hall.

Mahunkahme closed his eyes again and thought of Nemperara as she had been last night. The palace grand hall had been crowded for the festival to worship Amun and bring a great flood for the Delta. His four wives had sat surrounding him during the feast, his twelve children around them. All had been well with his priests united in assuring him the gods had never been more favoured to their land and its pharaoh.

Nemperara had sat at the far end of the great pharaoh's table. She was beautiful. Her black braided hair was cut to shoulder length, as was the fashion. Her emerald green eyes sparkled enticingly and he knew of no other with eyes the colour of the precious stones. Her smile was surely the most alluring in the land, the whiteness of her teeth offset perfectly by the olive skin of her face. Mahunkahme had been captivated by her since she had first entered his palace.

He could have commanded her to be his wife yet he ached for her to want him as much as he wanted her. He had her admitted into his household. At the last new moon she had travelled with him on his barge to the Festival of the Valley on the banks of the Thebes. His people had adorned his barge and the ground he walked with masses of flowers.

As the barge had been rowed back to the palace, with the setting sun and warm evening breeze, her presence was irresistible. He had not known such desire before. Alone for the first time, he had knelt before her and asked her to become his fifth wife. This was an honour no woman could dare dream of yet she had hesitated. However he was pharaoh and she had demurely agreed.

Mahunkahme had charged his brother, Amunkarnuk,

commander of the pharaoh's guard, to arrange the wedding festivities. Oh, how wrong he had been. He knew that now. Amunkarnuk had sat near her last night as they feasted. They had eaten together. They had laughed together, over and over. Pharaoh had watched the face of his wife-to-be for much of the night. He had burned for her, to hold her, to kiss her, to enter her. Last night more than ever. He had never seen a smile as alluring or enticing.

But she hadn't been smiling for Mahunkahme. It had been for Amunkarnuk. That onyx necklace told him everything. It was to have been his wedding gift to Nemperara, in the safe keep of his brother. The lined red stone, surrounded by the finest gold that he knew would glow on her chest. Yet it hadn't been him who had hung it there. It hadn't been him who had first witnessed that glow. He spat his brother's name out aloud. Amunkarnuk had taken the necklace and given it to Nemperara. That enchantress used her beauty to drive men from their minds—but she would not get away with this. Neither of them would.

'Pharaoh, my Pharaoh.' Ahmatuk stood before him, bowed, his face filled with apprehension. Mahunkahme had not even heard him enter the hall. He looked up, annoyed he had been disturbed but desperate to know where his brother was.

'He is nowhere to be found. The guard does not know where he is.'

Mahunkahme did not reply. He frowned, trying to think where his brother could be. His eyes opened wide and he leapt to his feet, his mind racing. He knew where his brother was; where they both were. There was only one way they could leave the palace unseen.

'Guard, my guard now.' He was yelling, his composure giving to the rage he had been suppressing.

The pharaoh was running now down the hallway, his spear-carrying guards scrambling to fall in behind him.

~ * ~

Amunkarnuk glanced toward the balcony, the sun high in the sky now, wondering if this would be their last day. The sky seemed perfect and he wondered why, if the gods wanted him

and Nemperara to be together, they were not helping to make it
so.

He looked at Nemperara. Her beauty had captivated him
since they met. How easily they talked together. How easily they
had walked the palace gardens together. He remembered how
he had knelt and picked a beautiful blue lotus flower and, as he
tucked it into her golden headdress, her hand had risen to touch
his forearm. Her eyes had wanted him, too.

Amunkarnuk looked at the bolted chamber door as excited
voices outside called loudly. It was clear what about. Both of
their names were amongst the maelstrom. The guard was
hunting them, no doubt led by Pharaoh himself. The little time
Amunkarnuk thought they had was gone.

He had grown up in this palace and knew every part of it
intimately. He did not want to die here now. He wanted to live
with his adored Nemperara.

The wall behind her had painted on it the most magnificent
team of black horses pulling a warrior's chariot. Standing in the
chariot was a fine archer poised to release an arrow into the air.

'Quickly, follow me now,' he ordered her. She had no idea
what he had in mind but clung to his hand. Amunkarnuk may
have lived here all his life, but for Nemperara the opulence of
the room was breathtaking. It seemed everything was made of
gold. Frames, bedheads, a table, even the giant door handles.
She had little time to take it in.

Amunkarnuk stood close to the mural, his eyes searching.
Fumbling for the right place, Amunkarnuk found what his hand
sought. The giant mural was their key for escape. The pharaoh's
bedchamber had a secret door and they had both run through it
many times as boys, when this was their father's room.

A small square of the wall gave way to the pressure of
Amunkarnuk's hand. The door swung open deceptively silently.
The tunnel beyond should have been dark, but instead there was
vague light within. Myriad hidden minor tunnels ingeniously
directed light from outside.

Amunkarnuk pulled her arm to follow. They ran into the
tunnel, her not knowing where they were going but with the
blind trust of one who faced certain death otherwise. The air
was musty and dank. Likely nobody had walked this passageway

since two little boys had done years ago. The tunnel was long and straight.

For Nemperara, escape was suddenly a possibility. Her fear of capture and death had given way to a lesser fear of where this tunnel went. She trusted Amunkarnuk and sensed he knew just what he was doing.

The tunnel was tilted downward, though not steeply. It narrowed as they ran and she brushed against the cold dampness of the stone. Without warning the tunnel ended and her heart rose in fear. There was no opening, no escape. Instead, before them, cutting them off from hope and safety, stood a wall. She forlornly knew now that her fate was indeed sealed, as Pharaoh's soldiers must follow them down to where they were trapped. She closed her eyes in prayer. Soon she would be with the gods and she wanted to make her peace with them quickly.

With her eyes shut she did not notice Amunkarnuk again running his hands over the wall. He knew what he sought, but could not remember where to find it. Frustrated, he pushed repeatedly until his fingers felt the cold resistance give way. The second door swung open, silently again. This time he had to shield his eyes as the full brilliance of the sun bore in on them. He took Nemperara's hand as they stepped out onto a flat-rocked area. Behind them the overgrown foliage on the rising cliff wall had helped conceal the perfectly sculpted rock doorway of the tunnel from outside eyes.

Nemperara's mouth fell open in awe at seeing the outside world again. Dare she believe they might survive yet to be together? Amunkarnuk surveyed where they were, seeing little different to when he last stood at this spot. They overlooked the mighty Nile and he could see traders and fishermen alike plying their way in either direction.

He spied what he had asked from the gods. A small, flat-bottomed cedar raft lay beached not far from where they stood. There was no mast, for indeed the owner would not intend to travel far. Likely this was for little more than crossing the enormous river. But it would serve their purpose handsomely. Two oars lay thrown onto its deck.

Amunkarnuk drew Nemperara in until their bodies pressed together. He was determined to keep her safe. He would die for her if he had to. Dying, though, was not part of his plan.

They had not yet made their escape. Amunkarnuk gently pushed Nemperara away from him and guided her down the steep ledge to the riverbank. There was nobody near the raft. Even if there had been, no person of this land would stand in his way.

He pushed the raft to the water's edge and held it steady as Nemperara climbed onto it. It was tied by a reed fibre rope. He stepped toward the stake and untied it.

'Amunkarnuk.' The voice called his name loudly and with the air of one used to command. It had an unmistakably sinister quality.

Amunkarnuk turned to his brother, chilled to find him so close. Mahunkahme had already climbed down from the ledge where the tunnel opened. He moved slowly, carefully. Voices could be heard to their left and right. Soldiers closed in on them, their prey certain. The pharaoh held a short, two-sided sword. There was little doubt he would use it. Fighting his brother might be inevitable for Amunkarnuk, but so too was their capture and death now.

'You have stolen my heart from me my bro ... ' The pharaoh's voice halted. He began again. 'No, you are no longer my brother. You are dead to me. As is that daughter of Seth.' He gestured the sword toward Nemperara.

Amunkarnuk stood silently still. He was unsure if he would fight or not. He needed to save Nemperara and that drove him to find some avenue for her escape. He prayed she would be able to row the raft fast enough with the help of the strong current—if she could escape the guard's volley of deadly arrows. Before that, though, he had to find a way to stop his brother. His eyes roamed the ground for a weapon of any kind. There was nothing, not even a stick.

Without warning the pharaoh suddenly lurched backward, falling heavily, his footing lost. A rock had given way, leaving him to slide the short way to the riverbank. The sword fell from his grasp and clanged loudly as it bounced off stones. For a moment neither of them moved, so taken by surprise that no reaction was instinctive. As the pharaoh tried to rise, his head jerked back, his eyes wide with a fear that Amunkarnuk had never seen in them before.

Between them rose the head of a giant cobra. It was easily as long as Amunkarnuk stood and had risen to at least half that height. Its hood flared menacingly. Its tongue flickered evilly. Its body arched back slightly in preparation to strike. It was too near to the prostrate pharaoh, who had no chance.

In an instant, Amunkarnuk acted. He rolled forward, coming up with the dropped sword firmly in his grasp. Even as the roll brought him back to his feet the sword sliced through the air. The arc was perfect and in an instant the head of the giant serpent lay by the feet of the pharaoh. The lifeless body fell to the ground, unmoving.

The two men stared into each other's eyes. Amunkarnuk held the sword, but for what purpose now? To have saved his brother, only to slay him to allow escape?

Voices broke their silence and soldiers ran to them, surrounding Amunkarnuk. Mahunkahme raised his arm and they all fell silent and motionless. Without standing, the pharaoh moved his eyes to his lost love, Nemperara. She was fearful of him. Amunkarnuk turned to face her and their eyes met. Her face changed completely. There could not have been more love coming from her gaze, nor from his brother to her. She had chosen.

The raised arm slowly gestured to the left and right. Soldiers hastened aside, leaving an opening to the raft. Mahunkahme pointed to his brother, then to the raft. His finger swept slightly, enough for Amunkarnuk to understand.

Perhaps for the last time, he faced his brother. Stepping forward, he turned the sword, handing the hilt to Mahunkahme. He bowed, stepping backward. The pharaoh stared at him then gestured to stand fast a moment. He reached into a pouch sewn into his dress. The onyx necklace appeared. For a moment the pharaoh eyed the beautiful stone before tossing it to his brother.

Amunkarnuk stared at the precious onyx now in his grasp then turned his eyes back to his brother. For a moment they stared at each other before he turned and took up the rope, slipping the raft into the water. Nemperara reached for his hand, steadying him as he stepped onto the raft. He raised her hand to his lips in a brief kiss as the raft moved away. Into her palm he placed the jewel, closing her fingers around it. Before he could even take up the oars, the strong current was already sweeping them down river to their life together.

Desire and the Divas
By
Imelda Evans

The rehearsal was not going well.

Even while still on the stairs, I could hear the merciless tones of a conductor on the warpath. By the time I had panted my way through the third floor door and halfway down the corridor, he was expressing himself in terms that would have attracted the attention of the Royal Society for the Prevention of Cruelty to Tenors, had such a society existed. (Sadly, nobody cared enough for tenors to start one.) Counting my lucky stars that I was a mezzo, I slid silently through the door furthest from the front of the rehearsal room and into my usual spot next to Anh.

'You're late,' she whispered.

'Not really,' I countered. 'Not compared to the tenor's entries, apparently.'

She smothered a giggle in her music folder.

'Serves our esteemed leader right for choosing a tenor for his looks instead of his musicality.'

'He can't help being gay!' I replied, too quickly, and immediately began fretting that I'd given myself away. I'd only been in the company a few weeks, and while Anh and I had bonded instantly, I was still in the 'don't ask, don't tell' stage with her. I know it sounds crazy, in 2017, to be worried about telling people that you're gay, but I'd only recently come to terms with it myself. I wasn't yet hardened to other people's reactions.

She patted my hand consolingly, without taking her eyes off

the conductor.

'Of course he can't help it, chook, but it's no excuse for letting his eyes overrule his ears. Especially for a brand new opera.'

I agreed, but I didn't get a chance to say so because at that moment the main door flew open and admitted someone who even I, an opera neophyte, could see was a bona-fide Diva.

I couldn't have explained what gave her such presence. She wasn't tall or thin, especially young or particularly beautiful—none of the things that women were supposed to be, to be worthy of attention. Nor were her clothes anything special. She was wearing black trousers, a black top, low-heeled black boots and a red chiffon wrap. The only really striking element of her ensemble was a huge onyx pendant resting on her magnificent cleavage. The necklace was a nice nod to the name of the opera—*The Onyx Affair*—but overall, the outfit wasn't likely to feature in the fashion pages.

Yet somehow, simply by walking in, she commanded the attention of everyone in the room. The conductor halted his tirade mid-insult and turned to welcome her. The tenor drew himself up to his full, not-very-impressive height and preened in a way that boded badly for the musical director's chances. The sopranos, Anh included, sighed in a mixture of admiration and envy.

As for me, I was transfixed. The tatty rehearsal room, the preening tenor, the conductor; they all receded and I was swept, helpless, into an attraction that felt totally new.

Except ...

It wasn't new at all, I realised, as the room spun around me, reforming my world with every revolution. I'd felt it before, but I'd never properly acknowledged it. Determinedly locked in a closet of my own fear, I'd denied all such emotions.

But now I was out and all those suppressed yearnings were boiling to the surface, released by this amazing woman, this Diva, who was so vibrantly present, so sure of herself, so gloriously, sexily, unapologetically, female—so different from everything I had spent years trying to convince myself I wanted. From her piled-up hair, as black as the onyx on her chest, to her neat, suede-encased feet, she exuded essence of woman—and my recently un-closeted libido wanted *all* of it.

Anh squeezed my hand and beamed.

'Thank God she's here! Now we'll hear some *real* singing!'

I turned to her but couldn't speak. I couldn't even breathe normally. Her hand on mine seemed to be the only thing stopping me from floating out the window into the night. Arranging syllables into sense was quite beyond me.

'Are you okay? You look a little odd.'

I felt odd. All my senses had been thrust onto high alert. Everything was magnified. The creak of Anh's leather jacket as she leaned towards me was a roar. My hand tingled where she touched me and the apple scent of her shampoo filled my nostrils to the point of making me light-headed.

'I think I'm in love!'

Her eyes opened wide and I realised, too late, that I might be giving too much away.

'With our resident coloratura?'

I backpedalled.

'No, of course not! That'd be mad, wouldn't it? It's probably just lust.'

Oh dear, that wasn't better.

'*Lust?* Well, well … I'm sure you're not the first. She's quite something, isn't she?'

Her smile had broadened to a grin. My face felt as if it was on fire.

'For her voice, I mean!' If I'd been backpedalling this hard on an actual bike I would have been down the six flights of stairs and out on the street by this stage, but I may as well not have bothered. I wasn't convincing myself, much less Anh.

'The voice you haven't heard yet …' She shifted back into her seat, so she could watch the conductor, but her eloquent side-eye said what her mouth didn't.

So much for not letting on! I was pretty sure she knew I was gay now. But it didn't seem to bother her. In fact, she looked … satisfied? Could that be right? It wasn't the reaction I'd been expecting, but it was better than many I'd feared. Maybe she'd suspected and this was her reaction to finding out she was right?

There was no time to ask though, even if I could have found the words. There was no time to talk at all. The Diva had come to rehearse with the chorus and the conductor was not about to let us disappoint her.

By the time we were released into the wilds of a cold, wet, Melbourne winter's night, I was exhausted from singing and dizzy with emotion.

I expected Anh to grill me as soon as she'd got me alone, but she didn't. She did drag me (physically) along to the post-rehearsal pub session, but once we were installed in our corner, she limited her conversation to the usual gossip about who was fabulous, who was flat, who was getting off with whom and who had ideas above their ability. (We agreed that the hapless tenor would not be in his current role for long.) The others had plenty to say about The Diva, but Anh took pity on me and even managed to divert anyone else from asking me questions about her. So I made it through the night with no revelations, no reactions and no repercussions. Exactly as I'd hoped and planned.

I couldn't decide whether I was pleased or disappointed.

~ * ~

The next three days passed in a daze.

I went through the motions: I got up, went to work, washed, ate and slept (sort of), but I wasn't really present for any of it. I was like a teenager with her first crush. In a way, I *was* a teenager with her first crush. All that repressed sixteen-year-old intensity had been shaken loose and it had knocked me sideways as thoroughly as a big wave at the beach, leaving me floundering in the surf, completely off balance and able to be toppled by the merest tap. A pretty face on the train would fling me headlong into a well of uncontrollable daydreams. Cute cat videos on Facebook could bring me to tears. And any glimpse of a clock had me counting the hours until the next rehearsal.

I had no idea how to deal with it all. I desperately needed guidance. But who could I talk to? I hadn't been in Melbourne long and none of my new friendships had got to the stage of love advice. Especially not gay love advice. I was out to my family but I was hardly going to talk to Mum or my brothers about *this*. And while some of my old friends knew, they'd barely had a chance to get used to the new me before I left for

Melbourne. How could I explain to them that I thought I was in love with a woman I'd never even met?

The person I really wanted to talk to was Anh. I hadn't known her long, but from the beginning I'd felt that she was the kind of friend you could say anything to—well, almost anything. Maybe it was time to break that last taboo. Surely she'd understand?

But … what if she didn't? She *was* half-Vietnamese. Her mum, by all accounts, was pretty strict and traditional. If I told her outright I was gay, would that mean she couldn't hang out with me? Maybe *that* was why she hadn't said anything after rehearsal. Not because she was sparing my feelings, but so she didn't have to know! Or was I just being racist? I hadn't met her mum. For all I knew she had 75 gay cousins and was a regular at the Pride Parade.

It was usually at this point in the mental raving that I decided that I should just ring her. Or text her. Or maybe write a letter. We spoke most days. If I didn't talk to her for three days straight, she'd wonder what was going on. But every time I went to press the button on the phone, I chickened out, hamstrung by my biggest fear.

What if she thought I wanted more than friendship from her? How on earth was I supposed to talk about my emerging gay love life with a straight female friend without it being weird? She was the kindest, sweetest person in the world, but what if it was too much for her? How would she deal? How would I?

And so it went. Around and around and around my head, at least once an hour during the day and several times during the night, as the days dragged on.

~ * ~

I was early for the next rehearsal. Early, carefully dressed and wearing makeup. I knew it was desperate and probably useless. The Diva wasn't likely to come to rehearsal again so soon. It wasn't as though she needed to. She was a pro. And she'd hardly be likely to notice a lowly newbie chorus mezzo, even if she did. But I hadn't been able to help myself.

This time it was Anh who sidled in just as rehearsal was starting. She looked amazing. She was wearing her favourite shade of purple, which made her skin glow without any need for makeup. But it was more than that. Her eyes were sparkling in the way they only did when she had a particularly delicious secret.

'What's up with you?' I said, as soon as she plumped down next to me.

'Nothing,' she replied. Her eyes didn't agree, though. Now that she was near, I could see that they were not so much sparkling as doing impressions of the entire night sky. 'You look nice.'

I blushed again, proving that I really was stuck in my teens.

'So do you, but don't change the subject. What are you hiding?' The irony of *me* asking that question of *her* did not escape me.

'You'll see,' she said, giving up the pretence, but not the information.

I could see that no amount of prodding was going to get any more out of her, so I gave up in favour of concentrating on the work at hand. Our conductor was a lovely man outside of rehearsal, but when it was singing time, he had a very low tolerance for chatting in the ranks. For the next hour, I had to content myself with sideways glances at the still-starry eyes and wondering.

Then, just before break time, the conductor himself let the cat out of the bag. Putting down his baton, he smiled and said, 'Before we go to break, I have an announcement to make. As you know, one of our usual guest sopranos will be singing the lead in *The Onyx Affair*, but she will need an understudy and we have decided to draw from our own ranks for that role. Anh, would you come forward please? A round of applause for our understudy Onyx Princess!'

To thunderous applause, Anh sashayed forward to stand next to him. But as she turned with an elegant swish of her skirt to receive her congratulations, my hands faltered and fell into my lap.

Physically, she was nothing like The Diva. She was tall, where The Diva was short; willowy, where The Diva was comfortably padded; and while The Diva was a flame-haired Scot, Anh's features and colouring owed much more to her

Vietnamese mother than her Australian father.

But that indefinable 'something' that had drawn every eye in the room to The Diva had now wrapped itself around my Anh and was flowing through her and reaching out to me the same way it had three nights ago. And I was responding exactly the same way. Except ... this time ... this time there was *more*.

With The Diva, I had been drawn to her confidence and vibrant femininity, had succumbed for the first time to a sexual attraction that I had never allowed to take hold of me like that before.

But with Anh it was different. The yearning was there. The rush of hormones twitching through my nervous system and churning up parts of me that were not used to tingling in that disturbing way. But this time the twist of sensation that started south of my navel rose all the way to my heart.

Three days ago, my desire had been an epiphany. Ever since, it had been a delicious distraction, a delightful daydream, only troublesome because I couldn't talk about it to anyone.

Now, I had a much bigger problem. It had taken a Diva to show me, but now that I could see I couldn't believe I had been so blind before. I *was* in love. But not with The Diva. I was hopelessly, completely, impossibly in love with my best friend. My straight best friend.

I bit my knuckles so as not to sob aloud.

Eventually, the applause died down and chatter took its place as people filed into the next room in search of tea and biscuits. By the time Anh had kissed all her wellwishers and come back to sit next to me, we were more or less alone.

'Good lord, girl, what's the matter? You look like you've seen a ghost!'

I could easily believe it. I could feel sweat beading on my forehead and my hands were trembling so hard I couldn't hold my music.

'I ...' I had no idea where to start.

She smiled at me and patted my hand, the way she always did. Except this time, it sent sparks shuddering all the way up my arm.

'You know ...' For a moment, she sounded almost as hesitant as me. 'I think I've seen you look like this before.'

'Really?' I couldn't imagine when.

'Yep. The other night, when you encountered The Diva. Do you remember what you said then?'

'Anh!' Why was she teasing me like this? 'It was three nights ago! Of course I remember!'

'You said …'

'I said I thought I was in love.' I didn't recognise my own voice, it was so squeaky.

'Or lust or something. Yes.' Her satisfied grin flashed out, then faded again. I dreaded her next question.

'Is that how you feel now?' For a soprano, her voice was surprisingly low and quiet. Sopranos usually don't have a quiet setting. It was one of the things I loved about her. Loved. Oh God. I did. I really did. And she was asking me if it was true. And I was going to have to tell her the truth. Even if it meant we couldn't be friends any more. I couldn't lie. I loved her.

'Yes.'

She looked deep into my eyes until I should have wanted to look away, but I didn't. I wanted to look into her eyes forever.

'Yes, you think you're in love?'

'Yes.'

'With my voice?'

'No.' Apparently I had lost the ability to speak in more than one syllable at a time.

'No?' Her eyebrows rose halfway to her hairline and her eyes glinted with mischief.

'Yes! But …'

'But?'

Time to stop messing about. I hauled in a shuddery excuse for a breath and took the plunge.

'I'm not just in love with your voice. I think I'm in love with *you*.'

Silence fell heavily over and around us. I stood it for as long as I could—it must have been several seconds—then rushed to fill it from my breaking heart.

'Of course, that doesn't have to mean anything. It won't destroy our friendship. You don't have to—'

She stopped me with a finger on my lips. Her own were curved in the satisfied smile again.

'You're a bit thick sometimes, you know that?'

And before I could protest or ask what she meant, she leaned in and replaced her finger with her lips. On mine. In a kiss. My first kiss from a girl. It was light and brief and sweet and new and it felt right. *So* right.

When she sat back, I found that the stars from her eyes had transferred themselves to mine. She was surrounded with starlight, which was pretty extraordinary in a room normally lit with flickering fluorescent tubes.

'Oh…' I was back to single syllables.

She took my hand and pulled me up.

'Come on,' she said. 'Let's get a cup of tea.'

So we did. Tea as black as onyx and as sweet as love.

It's not easy to make tea while holding hands with your new girlfriend.

But we managed.

Her Father's Gift
By
Caitlyn Lynch

Mina peered uncertainly into the big workshop. Various machines whirred loudly, sawing and grinding on stone, both men and women bending over them wearing aprons and safety goggles.

'Can I help you? I'm Val, the club president,' a pleasant voice said behind her, making her startle and spin around. She hadn't seen the older woman's approach.

'Well, I hope so. I asked the jeweller in town and he said that he couldn't help, but that I might find someone here who could.' She fished the small suede bag out of her pocket. 'These belonged to my father.'

'How unusual.' Val admired the gold cufflinks Mina spilled out into her palm. A coiled-rope design spiralled around a polished, opaque light green stone in one, but in the second, the gem was missing. 'Ah. And you're looking for a replacement stone?'

'Yes, if that's possible.'

Val smiled at her. 'You've come to the right place, dear. This is a lapidary club; I'm sure I can find someone who will take the job on.' Humming to herself briefly, she gestured for Mina to stay put before entering the workshop and approaching one of the men working at a grinding wheel.

The man glanced over his shoulder at Mina before nodding to Val and reaching to switch his machine off. Removing his goggles, he dried his hands on a towel before approaching with a smile.

A little surprised, Mina blinked at him before smiling back shyly. She'd expected the lapidary club members to be mostly older folks like Val, but this man couldn't be much older than her twenty-seven years, tall and nice-looking with short black hair and amber-gold eyes.

'Hi,' she said nervously.

'Hi, I'm Chris. Val said you need a replacement stone for a cufflink?' He had a lovely smile, bright in his tanned face. Mina couldn't resist looking at his hands as she held the cufflinks out for him to inspect. No wedding ring—though that might not mean anything, considering how easily it could be damaged using the stone grinding machines he was using, but she saw no tan line where one might normally be worn.

'They were my father's,' she explained, 'and his father's before that. I'm not sure exactly when the stone was lost from this one.'

'Okay, and you'd like a replacement stone? Planning to give them to your boyfriend?'

'No, I ... maybe? One day? If I get one?' He was checking her hands out for rings too, she realised, a rosy blush rising to her cheeks.

'I see.' Chris grinned at her. 'Thought maybe you were planning to turn them into a pair of earrings or something.'

The thought hadn't occurred to her, but she shook her head. 'No, I don't think so. I think I'd like to keep them as cufflinks. Maybe one day I'll have a son to hand them on to.'

'Okay.' He was still looking at her rather than the cufflinks, but at last turned his attention to the gemstone he would need to duplicate. 'Do you know what it is?'

She shook her head. 'I know that they came from Brazil originally. My grandfather was the Australian ambassador to Brazil for some years.'

'That makes sense, because I'm pretty sure it's Brazilian green onyx.' Chris moved away from the workshop a little to look at the gemstone in the sunlight.

'Onyx? I thought onyx was black!' Mina exclaimed, startled.

'Common misconception. Most so-called "black onyx" on the market is actually dyed. A lot of onyx is black with white banding, but it also comes in other colours. Like green or blue.

And I'm pretty sure that this is Brazilian green.'

'That's really cool,' Mina said, forgetting her nerves at being around such an attractive man in her enthusiasm. 'Will it be easy to replace?'

'The raw material is cheap enough. Most of the green onyx on the market is Chinese, though some comes from Iran. I've got a reliable supplier I can get some Brazilian from, though. It's cutting the stone that would be fiddly. It's an unusual cut.'

'It is?'

Chris smiled at her as she came to stand beside him in the sunlight, peering at the cufflink in his hand. The sun glinted off her brown curly hair, picked up red lights in it. She pushed wire-rimmed glasses up a pert little nose and looked up at him curiously.

'So what's unusual about the cut?'

'Er, yes,' he started, realising he was admiring her instead of focusing on the gem he was supposed to be assessing. 'Most faceted stones are cut with a point at the bottom and multiple facets on top to form what we call a pavilion. Like the diamond in a standard engagement ring.'

Mina nodded to show her understanding and Chris continued. 'Or you get cabochon stones, which are flat on the bottom and polished round and smooth on top. That's more commonly done with opaque stones—like black onyx, for example.'

'Right,' Mina looked at the cufflink again. 'But ... this one seems to be flat on the bottom, with a ... a *pavilion* on the top?' She checked that she had the correct term and he nodded.

'It's called a rose cut. Not seen very commonly at all, and no doubt why the jeweller sent you to us. It's not something you'd find in a gem dealer's inventory. It'll have to be specially cut.'

'Can you do it?' She had really pretty eyes behind her glasses, Chris noticed; large and blue, a hint of green in them. Long lashes swept down briefly and then back up again. 'If it's about money, I don't really care about the cost ...'

He chuckled. 'So I can charge whatever I like then?'

'Well, I wouldn't say that.' Mina smiled back at him for the tease. 'Within reason, I guess.'

'It won't be a fortune. The raw material is pretty cheap; I can get a slab as big as my hand for a few bucks. Probably a couple of hours to cut the stone, and since this is my hobby rather than my job, I don't charge huge rates for my time.'

'What is your job?' Mina asked curiously, then clapped a hand to her mouth. 'I beg your pardon. That was nosy of me.'

Chris grinned at her. 'It's okay, I don't mind. I'm a financial advisor.'

'Oh!' That explained the remark about charging huge rates for his time. If he was good at his job, he might very well charge hundreds of dollars an hour.

'Shall we say forty bucks?'

'But that's hardly anything!'

Chris chuckled. 'Well. Discount rates for a pretty lady.' His smile was warm and slow, making colour rise to Mina's cheeks again.

'Well,' she stammered out. 'If you're sure?'

'I'm sure. You hang onto these for now.' He pressed the cufflinks back into her hand. 'Give me your phone number and I'll call you once I've got the raw material in.'

'Okay.' He'd fished his mobile phone from the pocket of his jeans, looked at her expectantly, so she recited her number.

'And your name?'

'Oh—it's Mina.' Realising she hadn't introduced herself, she spelled it out. 'M—I—N—A.'

'Unusual name,' Chris commented, saving her details and putting his phone away.

'It's short for Wilhelmina, which is pretty ghastly. I was named after my grandmother.' She shrugged sheepishly. 'Everyone calls me Mina.'

'Can I call you, Mina?'

'Of course,' she blinked, confused. She'd just told him to, hadn't she?

'No, I mean ...' Chris shuffled his feet slightly. 'Can I call you? Not just about the stone. Maybe you'd, um, like to get coffee sometime?'

To her utter and complete astonishment, she realised that he was asking her out. Her blush, which had never really faded, came in with full force now. She was quite sure that she was scarlet to her hairline.

'Um. If you'd like to?' she stammered.

'Wouldn't have asked if I didn't.' He had a really nice smile, she noticed, flashing an unexpected dimple in his chin. She wanted to touch it, to trace her fingers over the six o'clock shadow growing in on his jaw, feel the rough texture scrape against the sensitive pads of her fingertips.

'Well.' Awkwardly, Mina took a step back. 'I guess I'd better be going.'

He didn't try to make her stay, but he did stay standing in the sun outside the workshop watching as she drove away, that smile on his face the whole time. Mina felt warm and tingly all the way home.

~ * ~

She really hadn't expected him to call as soon as the following night, but an unknown number popped up on her phone while she was cooking dinner. Expecting it to be a telemarketer, she was quite startled to hear Chris's deep voice saying hello.

'Uh, hello!'

'Am I being too eager?' He sounded amused. 'Only, I have a gap between appointments tomorrow morning and I was wondering if you'd like to get that coffee. Unless you're busy? You're probably working, I'm being an idiot ...'

'I'm a primary school teacher and it's school holidays,' she cut him off. 'I'd love to get coffee tomorrow.'

'Excellent!' He really did sound delighted. Mina couldn't fathom it, but she also couldn't wipe her own goofy grin off her face all that evening.

~ * ~

Chris was already at the coffee shop when she walked in the following morning. He looked up and smiled broadly as he saw her come in, standing up to greet her.

'You look different.' He cocked his head at her curiously before saying, 'Ah, no glasses!'

She smiled, taking the seat he gallantly held for her. 'I admit I was being lazy when we met. Couldn't be bothered to put my contacts in just to go to the lapidary club. I can't say that I expected to meet a cute guy who would ask me out for coffee.

Just goes to show that my mother really was right.'

'About what?' Chris cocked his head at her curiously.

'Well, she used to say that you should make sure you wear nice underwear every day just in case you have the misfortune to get hit by a bus, but I'm pretty sure the same principle applies.'

That made him snicker as he handed her the menu. 'Well. I won't ask if you put nice underwear on and I'll just be glad that you decided to wear your contacts, because you have really pretty eyes.'

'You too. I mean, your eyes are nice. Can you call a man's eyes pretty? They're a pretty colour anyway.' She was babbling, she realised, but she couldn't seem to shut up.

Chris smiled at her though, not seeming to mind that she was talking nonsense. 'Thank you.'

The waitress came to their table then and Mina ordered a latte. She shook her head when Chris asked if she wanted anything else, thinking that she was too nervous and would probably choke if she tried to eat. Her hands were trembling slightly and she suspected that she'd be lucky to escape without spilling coffee all over herself unless she could steady them.

'Tell me about how you got into lapidary as a hobby,' she asked, seeking a topic of conversation she hoped Chris would be comfortable with.

'My parents are both club members,' he told her, leaning back comfortably in his chair. 'They've been taking me out fossicking ever since I can remember.'

'Fossicking?' She looked a query at the unfamiliar term.

'Rock hunting,' Chris translated, grinning. 'My dad loves to tell everyone about the time I picked a five-carat sapphire out of a bucket of discards when I was five.'

She laughed at that, delighted. 'A prodigy!'

'My mum had it cut and set in a ring. She still wears it sometimes,' Chris told her. 'It's one of the best sapphires I've ever found, though I've got some nice ones I've yet to cut. I'll have to show you my rock collection sometime.'

'I'd like that,' Mina said enthusiastically.

Chris suddenly chuckled. 'Oh God—I just realised that totally sounded like an offer to "show you my etchings".' He waggled his eyebrows salaciously, grinning when she started to laugh, enjoying the joke. 'I do have some really cool rocks, though. I've got a beautiful Queensland opal I found last year, blue with just a trace of green in it. Almost exactly the colour of those pretty eyes of yours.'

She blushed, looked down at her hands. Relieved to see that they seemed to have stopped shaking, she said shyly, 'It sounds lovely. I'd like to see it.'

'I haven't polished it yet. Haven't decided what to do with it.'

The waitress returned then with their coffee and they settled into a comfortable conversation, Chris asking Mina what grade of primary school she taught. She found herself surprised by how relaxed he made her feel, comfortable talking about herself. She'd become a primary school teacher because she usually felt far more comfortable around children than adults. They were much less judgmental about her awkwardness.

The hour flew by and when Chris's phone beeped a reminder at him for his next appointment, she rose with a feeling of regret. 'This has been really nice. Thank you so much.'

'Thank *you*.' He stood as well, smiling warmly at her. 'I've really enjoyed it, Mina.' He ducked his head slightly and asked uncertainly, 'Maybe we could do it again sometime? Or … maybe you'd like to get dinner one evening?'

Mina was amazed to realise that Chris was just as lacking in confidence as she. She couldn't imagine how he could doubt her enthusiasm to see him again. She wouldn't leave him in any doubt, she decided. 'I'd like that very much. Saturday night?'

Chris managed to look simultaneously startled and delighted. 'Love to!' He suggested a nearby restaurant she'd heard good things about but never been to before they parted. Mina liked that he didn't suggest that he pick her up or that she go to his house; he was giving her space to get comfortable with him. A gentleman, she decided. Rare in the current day and age.

~ * ~

The first thing he said when she walked into the restaurant was, 'Your onyx came in yesterday!'

Mina smiled and took her seat, looking at the flat, palm-sized piece of stone he laid down on the table between them. It looked like an exact colour match to the one in her father's cufflink, even unpolished. 'That was quick.'

'Eh, I found it online and ordered it the day I met you.' Chris shrugged, looking a little abashed. 'Hoped I might impress you by being quick with the job.'

'Well, I'm impressed. You said you'd need the cufflink to match the sizing and cut of the stone though, and I don't have them with me.'

'Oh, no.' It was very clearly faux dismay. 'I'll have to see you again to get it!'

Mina laughed helplessly as he reached across the table to take her hand. Lacing her fingers with his, she said, 'I don't think I'll mind that at all.'

~ * ~

Six months later, Chris proposed to Mina with his mother's sapphire ring. He'd also commissioned a jeweller friend to make earrings for her, a match to her father's cufflinks, set with two more pieces of the green onyx. She gave him the cufflinks and he wore them proudly on their wedding day before they set off on their honeymoon—to Brazil, home of the green onyx stone that had brought them together.

Blind Date
By
Rosemary Pearse

The shadowed corners of Erica Duval's apartment crept towards her like a thief, stealing away her self-control, leaving her shaking, heart sprinting towards some non-existent safe space a million miles away.

Breathe. Erica's throat constricted and a strange, guttural noise escaped. The apartment was dark but for the bright light illuminating her workspace where straw, beading and feathers erupted in colour and texture.

'Too many shadows.' Erica scooted to the bank of light switches on the column in the open space of her converted warehouse apartment. Flicking the switches, light flooded the living area. With every light blazing and darkness banished, Erica repeated her mantra. 'I'm safe. I'm OK. I'm home.' Wrapping her arms around her body, counting backwards from twenty, the panic ebbed.

It wasn't often she got caught out like that. Flashbacks to the night she was stranded alone in a blackout—attacked, her bag stolen and no way to get home—were rare but powerful.

'Panic attacks won't help me get through this mountain of work.' The spring racing season was coming up. If she could pull it off, Erica would have her best year yet. Working late and pushing the limits meant the right people would be wearing her signature hats.

Spinning the plinth, Erica cast a critical eye over her efforts. Resting on the hat block was a broad brimmed, sixties-inspired black-and-white sun hat for a young actress on the rise. It was already stunning; a few more hours and Erica knew it would be spectacular. Worth every cent of the crazy money people were willing to pay for an Erica Duval original.

'I'm starving.' Erica rubbed at her tired shoulders. Fixing herself a snack with one eye on the clock, she was back to work by 10 pm. As the radio news finished, she turned the volume up and the familiar intro music of her favourite program floated across the airwaves.

'Down we go, my friends, right down low. Davis Lane with you again tonight as we push on down through the black to the Midnight Blue.'

The mesmerising sounds of Davis Lane. His rich, melodious voice was a gift. Five nights a week he spoke to her, only to her, kindling warmth in her heart, and she was a little less lonely, a little more brave. It wasn't the words; though they were wonderful, someone else could have spoken them. The tone of his voice resonated in her body, a perfect pitch, a tune curling around her like a warm hug on a cold night. His voice lit the darkest corners of her soul. She felt safe listening to him.

Davis Lane took Erica on journeys around the world, through the backwaters and backstories of little known musicians, newly discovered or long forgotten. Davis Lane knew them all. The passion he shared for the rare catalogues and musical remainders was a gift to his devoted listeners, but for Erica it was so much more.

If only he knew ...

She had once dreamed of an adventurous life, exploring the world, gathering inspiration and soaking in the experiences of other cultures, meeting strangers, venturing into the unknown. But her dreams and her real life were not compatible. She hadn't left her apartment in three years.

~ * ~

'Barbara Lewis, queen of the mid-tempo ballad, with a song she wrote for her debut album back in '63, *Hello Stranger*. It might have been way before I was a sparkle in my father's eye, but this song is a favourite of mine and it's going out to the lonely, the broken hearted and for anyone in a melancholy mood tonight.'

'Oh, Davis. You know me too well.' The song wove its

evocative magic across the airwaves.

Davis returned as the song faded, his voice bright with excitement. 'I have a special announcement tonight, a challenge with a prize you will promise your firstborn for.'

Erica stopped working, her interest piqued, tired eyes blinking in the casino-like brightness of her apartment.

'It's called Blind Date and it's going to be more fun than a frog in a glass of milk. If you are good at solving puzzles and ready, willing and able to join me next Saturday, you may be the lucky one to win a blind date … with me. Are you brave, music lovers? Will you take a chance on me?'

Her mind exploded in a million directions. A date with Davis Lane? The man who spoke directly to her heart?

'I must win. There's no other option. Nothing and no one can stop me.' Erica almost levitated with nervous energy. She paced in front of the radio, thinking aloud. 'Solving the puzzle will be easy. Leaving the apartment?' She groaned in dread. 'Not so easy.'

'Are you ready? If you are the first person to ring in with the correct answer tonight, dinner is on me. I promise you an entertaining and revealing evening of wonderful food and the best of company, but first you will need to solve the Midnight Blues Clues,' Davis's deep voice teased. 'Your two clues are coming up. Keep your ears peeled.'

Erica searched frantically for pen and paper. Her pulse raced and she broke into an instant sweat at the thought of meeting Davis Lane.

'Focus, c'mon. Focus!'

'Now, let's get to it. The first clue is a rare track from Onyx Records, an old doo-wop recording I discovered in a junk shop in New Orleans many moons ago. The Velours with Can I Walk You Home?'

Sweet melody and close harmonies wafted from the speakers, helping Erica to calm down. She scribbled: Onyx, doo-wop, New Orleans, The Velours, Can I Walk You Home? As the song played out, she added: music, junk.

'I hope you got all that, because here comes the second clue: the title of the Massive Attack and Tracey Thorn collaboration.' Davis was known for his eclectic taste in music. 'Let the clues lead you on your journey of discovery. Leave no stone unturned.'

'You're loving this, no doubt about it.' Erica beamed, her senses alive. 'And so am I.'

The music welled with haunting minimalism. Erica knew it well. She added the song title, Protection, to her list, underlining it. She added: journey, discovery, stone … love. She played with the words, looking for links as the track played out.

The music references were obvious but Erica was certain Davis would be more obscure. He wouldn't want a date with someone obvious.

No! He was a man of adventure, the road less travelled. My kind of man. Erica's eyes flared. She'd never met her kind of man. 'But I haven't met Davis yet, have I?'

Erica wrote a fresh list, omitting music references and focusing on the second clue: protection, onyx, junk, journey, discovery, love. 'That's more like it.' She crossed out junk; it didn't fit. Erica went to her computer and typed: protection onyx. Pay dirt.

Erica read aloud, 'Black onyx is a powerful protection crystal, aiding self-control, shielding you from negative energy, building inner strength and self-mastery.'

'Gotcha!' She trembled, her body on fire with anticipation. Dialling the radio station number, her fingers shaking and uncertain. Engaged.

'No!' She let loose a strangulated cry, urgent and furious. Could someone have the answer before her? She tried again. It rang … and he answered. 'You're mine.' The words shot out of her mouth before she could stop them.

'Nice to meet you, too. There's just the small matter of a correct answer.' Davis was amused but Erica was flustered.

'It's black onyx. I'm sure of it.'

'Well then, you were spot on. I am yours and I don't even know your name.' He sounded so sure, so confident, while Erica was as jittery as a kitten.

'Erica.'

'Are you ready for our blind date, Erica?'

'Not yet, but I will be.' In that moment, Erica knew. If anyone could get her out of her apartment, it would be Davis

Lane.

~ * ~

Erica placed one foot in front of the other, talking herself through her panic until she was inside the restaurant. The maître d' showed her to the table, but seeing Davis sitting there, gazing into the distance, she stopped dead in her tracks. His profile was compelling: a swimmer's broad shoulders, short dark hair and a generous mouth. He was not straight-out handsome, but there was humour and kindness in his lived-in face.

Davis sensed her presence and sprang from his chair, beaming in her direction. His smile almost knocked her over. A parade of emotions danced across her face.

'Erica! Congratulations.'

She'd know his voice anywhere and it sounded even more magical in real life.

Davis held out his hand and she placed hers in his. The strength of his grip eased her nerves. When he placed his other hand on top, sealing their touch, a warm buzz filtered through her veins. He leant forward, as if to tell her a secret or to give her a kiss. Unsure of his intentions, Erica threw caution to the wind, leant forward and planted a kiss fair on his cheek.

Davis pulled back as if in fright and all that sweetness flew away. Erica's heart launched into a complex rhythm sequence. Though her kiss was nothing more than a passing glance, she was close enough to smell the delicious concoction of man and soap. She drank him in and her rollercoaster anxiety dipped.

'I'm sorry,' Erica laughed nervously, feeling embarrassed. 'I wasn't sure …'

'Please don't apologise.' Davis beamed, his smile a little crooked but full of character. He reached for the back of his chair, gesturing towards the empty seat opposite his. 'It's been a while since someone has stolen a kiss from me.'

'I've never stolen a kiss. From anybody. I'm so …' Erica stopped herself. In a heartbeat, she knew it was time to stop being so afraid. 'You know what? I'm not sorry at all. I'm thrilled to meet you and there's no harm in a simple kiss, is there?' Adrenalin surged through her veins. Erica checked herself, wanting to head off any panic attacks at the pass. But I feel good. I'm safe, I'm OK and … goddammit, I feel happy. Like a kid with a secret, she was fit to burst.

'No harm at all.' He smiled, his tone reassuring, genuine. 'Would you like a drink?' Davis gestured to the waiter standing close by, ready to take their order.

Conversation flowed throughout their meal. Davis was charming and Erica delighted as each word, spoken only for her, filled her in a way the wine and food never could. Erica blossomed in the warmth of his attention, like a rare hothouse orchid. She felt beautiful and brave.

'I have a confession.' Erica's impulse to share her secrets with Davis overrode any remaining fear and anxiety. 'Tonight has been so much more to me than a blind date.' She couldn't look at him in case she lost her nerve and panicked mid-word. 'I've been avoiding my own life. I'm petrified of the dark but I've been living under a rock. I stay home in case I fall apart, but instead the four walls of my apartment have become my prison. But you were my light in the darkness, your stories, the music … you were always there for me.' Waves of emotion washed over her. This confession, this intimacy between them was dreamlike and surreal, but the words flowed from her. 'And now you've changed everything. You unlocked the door and freed me. To say thank you … it doesn't seem enough.' A weight fell from her heart, dissolving into thin air, and she was free.

Erica searched Davis's face for understanding and compassion. Instead she found him looking over her shoulder as though she wasn't even there. Was he bored? She'd been so caught up in the rush of her own emotions.

An uncomfortable silence stretched out between them. 'I'm sorry. Did I say too much?' Erica's face flushed with a wave of indignation. She'd made a terrible mistake. Fear rose in her throat like an incoming tide, drowning her.

Davis emptied his glass of wine and took a deep breath. 'I love what I do. It's helped me … more than you could know. I can't tell you how much it means to me that Midnight Blue has meant so much to you.' The tone of his voice had changed. It was husky, as though there was more air carrying his voice to her.

Erica lost feeling in her hands. Her heart could not take much more. Her ears buzzed with the blood throbbing through her head. This sounds like goodbye.

He refused to meet her eye, looking to the left of her face and then off to the right. Never quite looking at her. Real life had struck and Erica, unable to move, feeling like she was about to throw up, was devastated. Still, he looked straight past her.

'Erica?' His voice soft. 'What colour are your eyes?' His beautiful mouth curled into the question, half smiling. His voice teased her. 'Your hair?'

Erica frowned, confused. He squinted in her direction, moving his head as if searching for a hidden target.

'You will have to tell me, if I'm ever to know, because I'm not sure you've noticed, but … my vision is … I can't see too well.' His casual words were spoken without weight or drama. 'It's macular degeneration … I've had it for a while, gradually losing my sight, and now … I'm legally blind.'

Erica sat in shocked disbelief.

'I've got a small amount of vision left, mostly peripheral. No dog, no cane, pretty good on spatial awareness and object perception. Working on the echolocation.'

'Oh, I see …' Erica could have been launched into outer space and been less surprised.

'Well … you do, but I don't.' Davis chuckled and Erica groaned. 'I meant to tell you earlier, but … there's no easy way. Besides, you were telling me how spectacular I was and I didn't want to interrupt you.' His light banter took the edge off the situation.

'I'm so sorry. I had no idea.' Erica was embarrassed. She'd been so self involved, she hadn't seen the man sitting right in front of her.

'Nothing to be sorry about. It's just how it is.' Davis shrugged and grinned. 'I was doing pretty well for a while there. I'm not too bad at faking it.'

Davis held his hand out for a high five and Erica placed her hand against his, feeling his welcoming energy and entwining her fingers between his, holding on.

'You are amazing at faking it.' She squeezed his hand, sending a smile to him in her touch.

'I hope you're not.' He smiled and squeezed back. The intensity of the moment burst with their laughter.

Erica blushed, thankful he could not see it. Her pulse raced and her chest exploded with colour, with light and the spark of passion. Davis's whole body had relaxed and his face lit up with sassy delight.

'I thought you hated me. I thought I was boring you.' Erica collapsed back into her chair, relief washing over her.

'Hey, I saw that.' Davis joked and Erica sprang back, a guilty look on her face. 'Ha! I'm only joking. I really am blind.'

'Ahhh … so it really was a blind date. For both of us.'

'It sure was.' Davis took a deep, satisfied breath. 'It's been the best night I've had in a while, thanks to you. But now I'm going to officially finish this date. I've met my commitment for the station. I'm clocking off.'

'Really?' Her disappointment stung. She busied herself collecting her belongings, hiding her hurt.

'But now that I'm off duty, I was hoping we might take a stroll together?'

Air flooded back into her lungs, life back into her veins. 'I'd love that.'

Erica marvelled as they walked together, moving through the Saturday night crowds. Davis was fearless despite being blind and his strength wrapped itself around her. The darkness, the strangers on the street, were no longer threatening with him walking beside her.

'I have something for you.' Davis slowed and stopped by a softly lit store window. Reaching into his jacket pocket, he produced a tiny box.

'Oh, Davis!' Erica mocked. 'We might need to go on a few more walks before I can marry you.'

Davis laughed as he opened the box and picked up the polished gemstone inside. 'Black onyx—for protection, strength and determination.' Davis reached into his trouser pocket and produced another of a similar size. 'It's my talisman, my luck. Call me superstitious, but I like its weight, the smoothness. It calms me down and I like to think it keeps me out of trouble.'

Davis took Erica's hand in his and placed the onyx in her palm. 'This one's for you.' He folded her fingers around it and brought her hand up to his lips. 'I bought it as a memento for my blind date.' He turned her hand over and kissed the delicate skin of her wrist.

Erica felt as though she was suspended in honey, every moment drawn slowly through the amber syrup. As he kissed her fingers, his lips so warm and soft, Erica felt herself falling. Not for a voice, not for an illusion, but for the man standing in front of her. She pulled him closer, her hands finding their way around his sinuous arms, his pounding chest, his sensitive neck. Shaky and precarious up on her toes, she whispered into his ear. 'My eyes are the colour of a tropical ocean, my hair ... black coffee.'

Davis gathered her in, exploring her face with his gentle lips, finding her mouth with his. She breathed him in, every exquisite moment a delirious pleasure, alive with possibility.

'C'mon, trouble. Black onyx won't save me tonight.' Davis took Erica's arm and she led him into the night and onto her own real life adventure.

Keepsakes
By
Jane Newton

Sydney, 1899

'One onyx and pearl mourning ring, one yellow-gold mourning brooch—with your husband's hair set behind a glass frame.' David finished writing the order in the ledger and nodded to Mrs Fisher. 'We'll have that ready for you within the month.'

Mrs Fisher dabbed one eye with a lace-edged handkerchief. 'Thank you, Mr Goldstein.'

'Do you have Mr Fisher's hair with you?'

'Oh, yes.' The elderly widow dug into her silver mesh purse, produced a piece of folded paper and handed it to David.

He looked inside and took careful note of the rusty lock of hair, interspersed with threads of white. Thomas—his apprentice—looked over David's shoulder.

'I'll take this into the workshop immediately. Thomas, could you please see Mrs Fisher out while I lock this in the safe?'

'Of course.'

'Once again, I'm terribly sorry for your loss, madam.' David refolded the paper.

Mrs Fisher sniffed as Thomas walked around from behind the glass display case towards the front door.

David entered the small, dark workshop and heaved a sigh of relief. This commission should see them through until Christmas, when they would have to close for several days— even though he didn't celebrate the holiday. The last ten years had been a terrible time to be in business. He would be glad to see the new century ushered in.

He scrawled Mr Fisher's name on the paper and then reached up to the hook where the safe key should be. It wasn't there.

As he hunted about on the cluttered workshop bench, the bell rang, indicating that someone had entered via the rear door. David glanced at the clock: exactly four. It would be Sarah. Blowing out a frustrated breath, he continued to move tools and papers about on the bench. He heard footsteps in the hall.

He was finding it increasingly difficult to conceal his feelings for Sarah, but he couldn't let her see how she affected him. She could never accept him. They were too different; the disparity in their cultural backgrounds and temperaments would make happiness between them impossible.

'It's only me.' Sarah's cheerful voice rang out in the hallway and David frowned as he unlocked the workshop door. Sarah taught at the local school. After the students had left for the day and she had tidied up and prepared for the next day's lessons, she always came in via the back door to wait in the workshop while her younger brother, Thomas, finished work.

Sarah burst into the room, exuding her usual sunny effervescence in spite of her drab schoolmistress garb and no-nonsense reddish-blonde bun.

His stomach executed the ridiculous somersault it invariably performed whenever Sarah entered the workshop. He turned to nod to her. The Persian cat from one of the townhouses along the rear lane followed her inside, winding around her long black skirt and leaving a trail of white fur across it and the rug. Sarah bobbed down to pat the cat, then straightened and grinned at David.

His face turned crimson and he quickly focused his attention on the workbench.

'Have you lost your key again?' There was a smile in her voice.

She always seemed to catch him at the worst moment. Most likely she thought him foolish. He tried to keep the frustration out of his voice. 'Yes, but it's here somewhere. I used it this morning.'

She laughed and came to stand beside him. He tried to ignore the smell of rosewater on her soft skin, as well as the way her proximity heated the air. Did she have to stand so close? The day was already warm. His face was no doubt an alarming shade of puce.

Within seconds, she located the key and held it out to him.

'Thank you, Sarah.'

She caught him for a second with her steady, amused gaze. He forgot what he was supposed to be doing.

She nodded towards the metal wall safe and he blew out an exasperated breath. She must think him an utter imbecile.

The bell for the rear door sounded again and he put the key back down. 'That will be the gem merchant.'

Sarah smiled and made her way to her usual chair in the far corner of the workshop as David opened the door for the merchant. The cat jumped up onto Sarah's lap.

The gem merchant bustled in. 'Hello, Mr Goldstein.'

'Hello, Mr Fein.' David hastily cleared a space on the workbench and gestured to it.

Mr Fein placed a large box on the workbench. 'I've had a fabulous shipment of diamonds this week. Are you in need of diamonds?'

'Not today, Mr Fein. I'm after a good-sized piece of black onyx if you have it.'

'Mourning jewellery, is it?'

He nodded. Fein opened the box carefully and removed the top layer, which was divided into compartments containing different gemstones. He picked up various envelopes that sat underneath, reading the labels and then casting them quickly to one side. Finally he found the one he wanted and opened it.

'Here we are: a beautiful piece of onyx. Will this do?'

David examined the gleaming black oval-shaped stone. It was the perfect size. He held it up to the light.

Sarah breathed out slowly. 'Oh, it's lovely, isn't it? I've never seen anything so beautiful. What a shame you need it for such a sombre purpose.'

David dropped his hand to his side and stared at her. How was he supposed to bargain the gem merchant down now?

Fein grinned at David.

'She knows nothing about onyx,' David said quickly. 'Sarah, perhaps you'd like to go into the shop to say hello to your brother. If it's quiet he can go home early once I'm finished out here.' And if she was gone, David could think straight.

She jumped up and walked towards the shop. She nodded to Fein and to David before disappearing through the door.

~ * ~

An hour later, as David prepared to lock up the shop, he suddenly remembered Mr Fisher's hair. He needed to put it away in the safe. After five minutes, he had found the key but saw no sign of the paper he'd scribbled on. He looked all over the bench, underneath it, and even turned the shop upside down looking for it. The paper—and the hair it contained—had vanished.

With dread thudding in his gut and rising up towards his chest, David closed the shop and went upstairs for the evening.

As he prepared his simple evening meal, he contemplated options for solving his predicament. One idea came to the fore, and he grimaced as he anticipated speaking to Sarah about it tomorrow.

~ * ~

'You want a lock of my hair?' Sarah arched a brow. 'I had no idea you felt that way about me—or that you were so sentimental.'

David rolled his eyes to the ceiling and huffed. 'Were you listening when I explained the problem?'

She chuckled and playfully tapped his arm. 'It's all right, David. I'll do it. I understand. So is my hair exactly the same shade as poor Mr Fisher's?'

She shouldn't be so familiar with him. He didn't think he'd invited that sort of informality.

Sarah removed the pins from her hair and began to unwind it. Her strawberry-blonde tresses glowed under the gas lamp. David caught his breath and tried to ignore his thundering heart. 'It's not exactly the same shade, but it's extremely close—as close as I'm going to find, I think.'

She smiled good-naturedly. 'And you'll mix it with cat fur?' she confirmed, bending down to pat the Persian lazing at her feet.

'Yes, luckily he's shedding so much in this heat. We won't need to give him a haircut.' David was relieved that Sarah had agreed to help. As Mr Fisher had been buried, there was no way of obtaining another hair sample. And he couldn't bring himself to tell his loyal customer he had lost it. Even so, his stomach churned when he thought about the deception—and about involving Sarah.

She ran her hand along the cat's back and clenched her fist, and then opened it to reveal a ball of white fluff. After placing it on the bench, she picked up the ends of her hair and leaned towards David. 'You should cut it. You know exactly how long it should be—and how much you need.'

He nodded and picked up the scissors. He closed his eyes before leaning closer to Sarah. His other senses took over, his nose filling with her scent and his skin growing warm from her nearness.

He opened his eyes and saw her watching him intently. She tilted her head to the side and then leaned forward—not in one smooth motion but haltingly, as if asking his permission before edging closer each time.

When her lips were within a few inches of his own, David closed the remaining distance and kissed her. It was something he'd dreamt of doing countless times, but hadn't dared believe she might want him to. Her mouth was as soft and warm as he'd always imagined it would be. He let the scissors clatter to the floor and pulled her closer with both arms.

He held her against him, her soft curves melding with the ridges and concaves of his body. Inexplicably, elation rose up within him—along with clamouring desire. They shouldn't be doing this here, with her brother in the next room.

David started to pull away, but Sarah stopped him. She weaved her fingers through his hair, massaging his scalp. He moaned against her lips. They shouldn't be doing this, but now he couldn't seem to stop.

~ * ~

Sarah eventually pulled back and smiled sheepishly at David. Had that really happened? She'd been daydreaming about him kissing her like that for so long. She inhaled and breathed in the familiar smells of the workshop that she associated with him: the oil that he used on the machinery, the tangy scent of metal that always hung in the air.

David walked towards the workbench and ran his long-fingered hands through his hair. 'I'm sorry. I shouldn't have done that.' He turned back to face her and there was worry in his dark eyes.

She stepped quickly after him. 'There's no reason why you shouldn't have.'

His eyes clouded with confusion now. He shook his head.

The sound of loud chatter filtered through from the shop. He turned towards it and looked at Sarah apologetically.

She waved a hand, urging him to go. She knew business had been quiet. A pre-Christmas rush—even a small one—might help her brother keep his job into the new century.

She flopped down onto the chair in the corner, embarrassed. Had she behaved badly? Thrown herself at David when he clearly wanted to keep her at a distance? Of course he'd responded to her advances—he was a man after all—but it seemed he'd immediately regretted his actions.

He hadn't taken a lock of her hair as he'd intended to. Sarah rose and retrieved the scissors. As she did so, she saw a small corner of paper sticking out from under the tatty Oriental rug. Prising it out, she found a folded piece of paper with the name *Mr Fisher* scrawled across it. When she carefully unfolded the paper, she found a lock of red hair shot through with white.

Sarah folded the paper back up again. She found the piece of onyx David had been working on, lifted it up and then used it as a weight to hold down the paper. Glancing through the open door to the shop, she saw David and Thomas attending to a small cluster of customers. She resolved to walk home alone, not wanting to see the regret in David's eyes again.

~ * ~

During the next few weeks, Sarah stopped going into the shop to wait for Thomas. She used the excuse that she was busy with final examinations. Then once school finished for the year, she didn't need to make excuses.

On Christmas Eve, Sarah had agreed to meet Thomas and

walk with him to their aunt and uncle's in town. She spent much more time than usual on her appearance, knowing she would be seeing David again. She didn't want to impress him; she merely wanted to show him how well she was coping in spite of his rejection.

Even so, her heartbeat thudded wildly and her breath hitched as she entered the workshop via the rear door, which had been unlocked for her. She'd hoped David would be busy in the shop, but he was seated at the workbench, his attention on the onyx and pearl ring he was polishing.

Forgetting that she had wanted to avoid him, Sarah stepped over to the bench to get a closer look at the ring. When she saw it, she drew in a sharp breath. 'It's exquisite. You've done beautiful work—as always.'

He turned to look at her. 'Thank you.'

She couldn't help noticing that his broad shoulders were slightly slumped and there were dark circles under his eyes. 'I'm sure Mrs Fisher will appreciate your efforts.'

David reached across the bench. 'She's coming to pick up the ring this afternoon—along with this, which thanks to you really does contain her husband's hair.'

She smiled and looked down at the gold brooch, which contained two perfectly arranged flourishes of hair, as well as tiny leaves and flowers. She looked up to meet David's dark gaze, struggled to find breath for a moment, and then inhaled deeply. 'What a lovely keepsake for her to remember her husband by. Were they together for very long?'

David nodded. 'Nearly fifty years. They emigrated during the early days of the gold rushes.'

'She must have loved him a great deal. How heartbreaking to lose him.' Sarah wanted to snatch those words back. Perhaps David would think she was silly and sentimental—or worse, still trying to throw herself at him. She straightened up. 'I've come to take Thomas to dinner at my aunt and uncle's, when he's ready.'

David put down the ring and the brooch and stood up suddenly. 'He's almost done. He's just tidying up the shop and then he can go. I ... I hope you have a nice Christmas.'

'Thank you. I hope you have a nice day tomorrow.' Sarah's

cheeks grew warm as David scowled. She had said the wrong thing again.

He shifted from one foot to the other. 'I've been wishing that ...'

Sarah bit her lip a moment, then released it and attempted an encouraging smile.

'I've been wishing I hadn't behaved the way I did a few weeks ago.'

She felt her face fall. 'Oh no, please. It was my fault entirely. You didn't do anything wrong. I shouldn't have—'

'Yes, you should have, or I should have long ago. At the very least I should have told you how I felt.' David shrugged.

'Please go on,' she urged. 'I'm listening.'

The door to the shop opened and Thomas looked through. 'Oh, you're here, Sarah. I'll be with you shortly. Mr Goldstein, Mrs Fisher has arrived.'

Sarah smiled at her brother and then turned to David. 'Go. I'll wait here.'

David gathered up the onyx and pearl ring, and the gold brooch containing Mr Fisher's hair. He walked to the door and paused, turning to smile at Sarah before he left. A surge of warmth flooded through her and settled low in her stomach when she saw that smile.

After she took her usual seat in the corner, she clasped her hands together and then laid them separately in her lap. She sat up straight and then leaned back more casually in the chair. A clock she didn't recognise—probably one brought in for repairs—ticked haphazardly on the wall.

She blew out a breath and shot to her feet. When it seemed like David might never come back through the door she stepped towards it. She had to go through. Maybe he had decided to leave through the street-facing door.

Just then the door opened and David returned. He smiled at her uncertainly. 'Mrs Fisher was very pleased.'

'That's good. Would you ...' Sarah's palms were warm and sticky with sweat. She brushed them against her skirt. 'Would you come to dinner with us? At my aunt and uncle's?'

David started to shake his head.

'It's not a very organised affair. She serves food on a side table and we stand around or sit and eat informally. She invites relatives, neighbours, my uncle's colleagues. You'd be most welcome.'

He gave a hesitant nod and Sarah's stomach cartwheeled. She'd experienced a similar sensation once when her father had sped over an incline on a country road in the buggy.

'You could come as Thomas's guest—' she dropped her gaze to her hands before looking up again '—and mine.'

'Thank you. I'd love to.' He glanced down at his suit and brushed at the fabric absently. 'Should I change? Or bring something along?'

She smiled and shook her head. 'You look perfect, and my aunt will have enough food to feed the whole of Sydney.'

'All right then.' He extended his hand towards her.

Her smile stretched into a broad grin. Her happiness was mirrored in David's face as she stepped forward to take his hand. He pressed his lips to hers, tentatively at first and then with more confidence, his touch spreading warmth through her.

When Thomas caught sight of them walking into the shop, hand in hand, he didn't comment on it. David's face was flushed, but he didn't drop Sarah's hand.

The three of them stepped out onto the bustling street. After Thomas locked the door, Sarah linked arms with each of the men: her brother and the man she had begun to see a shared future with.

The Onyx Rose
By
Kat Colmer

'How much are these red ones with the massive yellow semen?'

Eve all but dropped the bucket of tulips she was hauling out of the cool room and whipped her head around to see what the middle aged guy in the badly fitted suit was talking about.

'Stamen. The word you're looking for is *stamen*.' She shook her head. You'd think working at a flower shop would be low on the sleaze factor, but sleaze was kind of unavoidable when the shop was on the same block as a strip club and the Toys for Big Girls and Boys adult entertainment store. 'They're twenty dollars a pot.'

Gaze see-sawing between the flamingo flower with the admittedly impressive stamen and the cooling cabinet holding the more expensive onyx rose he'd first asked about, the badly-fitted-suit sucked air through his teeth while deciding.

'I'll take the stamen.'

No surprise there. They always choose the cheaper option.

He pulled out his wallet and flipped it open with a move that was all arse and no class. 'Something to remind the little lady of me, if you know what I mean.'

Eve ignored his comment, as well the creepy accompanying wink, and went about ringing up his purchase. She'd had enough of men who appeased their guilt after a stint at the seedy club with a bunch of flowers for the wife or girlfriend. In her experience, it wasn't long before guys like badly-fitted-suit ended up sticking their 'stamen' where it didn't belong.

Don't go there! You need to quit wasting time fuming over your dickwad ex-boyfriend and concentrate on the positives in life.

Like Miriam hiring Eve before she had even graduated from her horticulture science degree. Eve loved her job almost as much as she loved the mother hen shop owner who'd taken her under her wing when she'd needed it most.

Although Miriam's praise for Eve's work was constant, the Turkish-born florist also lamented the long hours Eve spent at the shop. 'Böyle bir atık,' she'd mutter under her breath. *Such a waste.* 'Enough work. You go dancing with nice young man. Move your curls!'

Curves. The word Miriam had been looking for was curves. But unlike badly-fitted-suit guy's vocab fumble, Miriam's brought a smile to Eve's lips—especially when the older woman insisted Eve was a flame-haired incarnation of none other than the Queen of Curves, Marilyn Monroe.

As for nice young men—ha! As far as Eve was concerned, nice young men had died out, driven to extinction by the likes of her ex and their stamen-loving egos. Besides, she didn't dance. There was a reason she loved flowers; they didn't require her to step out from behind her worktable and into the extroverted limelight her flame-red hair and look-at-me body led everyone to believe she craved. The last time she'd stupidly shaken her generous booty she'd ended up saying yes to her waste-of-space ex. So the safety of flowers it was. It meant little chance of meeting someone who, like her, preferred flower shops over strip clubs, but then Eve had given up on a genuinely nice guy walking into her life anyway.

The shop door creaked on its hinges, pulling Eve from her downward spiralling thoughts. The guy who stepped through wore his charcoal grey suit way better than her previous customer. He also rocked a pair of Clark Kent glasses, the top of which kept a swathe of scotch-and-Coke coloured fringe falling into the eucalyptus green-blue of his eyes. He lacked the air of sleaze badly-fitted-suit guy had wafted in on, but Eve stayed wary nonetheless.

'Hi.' He offered an innocent enough smile. 'I'm hoping you can help me. I'm after a bunch of flowers.'

No shit, Sherlock! I'd never have guessed! Eve cringed as soon as the nasty thought surfaced. Miriam was right; she was way too jaded for a twenty-three year old.

She forced a smile in return. 'Well, you're in the right place. What were you after?'

He glanced around and scratched the almost-but-not-quite five o'clock shadow peppering his jaw—his admittedly nicely-sculpted jaw. Not that Eve was paying attention or anything.

'That's the thing. I've got no idea.'

Eve took a breath. *This could take a while.* 'Who are we buying for?' He looked to be only a couple of years older than her, so unlikely to be married. Guilt flowers for a girlfriend then.

'They're for my mum,' he said with another smile, sadder this time. 'She's recovering from a round of chemo, so maybe something bright and cheerful?'

Eve didn't quite know how to respond, partly because she wasn't expecting flowers for his *mum*, but also because of the sadness hovering around the edges of his smile. She knew exactly where this guy was at right now; she'd walked in his shoes less than two years ago.

She swallowed the lump forming in her throat and forced some spark into her expression. 'Bright and cheerful. I can do that.' Lots of yellows and violets and pinks, that's what she reached for. Sunflowers and tulips and ... 'Peonies. I'll add some peonies.' She held up one of the pink rose-like blooms to show him. 'They're for healing.'

His 'thank you' flashed warmly in his gaze a second before he spoke the words.

She had no business asking but, 'How many rounds has she had?'

His eyes widened at the question. 'This was her second. They caught it early, which is good, but the nausea, it's just ...' He sent a shaky hand into the scotch-and-Coke waves of his hair. 'I work at the university a few blocks from here. I passed your window and thought flowers would brighten her day.' His gaze swept the shop, then came back to rest on Eve, the green-blue looking more than a little lost.

Somehow Eve managed to stop herself from reaching out and placing a hand on his arm. She nodded instead. 'Small, frequent meals help. It's worse on an empty stomach.'

Surprise flashed across his features.

She shouldn't have said anything; it wasn't her place. 'And these. These should help, too.' Avoiding the questions in his eyes, Eve held out the wrapped bunch of flowers to him.

He smiled a thank you again and paid for the arrangement.

Eve's gaze was still on the door he'd gently closed behind him when Miriam appeared from the cool room. 'Now, there.' She waved a soil-streaked hand at the shop entrance. 'He nice young man.'

Eve rolled her eyes at the older woman and busied herself cleaning leaves and stem cuttings from the counter. But maybe, just maybe, the Nice Guy species hadn't died out quite yet.

~ * ~

Not more than a week later, Eve found herself across the counter from scotch-and-Coke hair guy once again. This time he wore a snug fitting T-shirt, beneath which he was decidedly less Clark Kent and way more Man of Steel. Not that Eve was checking him out or anything.

'My mother loved the flowers,' he told her, a smile blooming across his face.

'So you're back for some more?' Because it wasn't like he had any other reason to come back to the shop now. Did he?

'Yeah, she enjoyed them so much I've decided to make it a weekly gesture.'

He'd be back weekly? A surge of something sweet shot through Eve's blood. 'That's great!' For business. Nothing more.

Ha! You keep telling yourself that.

Eve cleared her throat. 'The same arrangement or something different?'

'The same for Mum, thanks.'

Eve nodded and turned for the sunflowers.

'But I'm also after a second bunch, one that says something along the lines of, "you're too good for him."'

Eve's hold on the flower stems slipped a little. 'Trying to win someone's heart?'

His throaty laugh bounced off the shop's walls and landed smack at the bottom of Eve's belly. 'No.' He shook his head. 'The second bunch is for my sister. Her boyfriend dumped her and, well ... I'm doing my big brother bit to help her get over the guy.'

'Oh.' First his mother and now his sister? Maybe Miriam was right and Eve was looking at the last of the Nice Guy species.

She took a breath. 'Well then, you'll want bold, vibrant colours. Waratahs, wild orchids and ...' she looked around until her gaze fell on exactly the right flower. 'Foxtail lilies. Definitely foxtail lilies. For perseverance.'

'Perseverance. That's perfect.' His smile spread slowly across his features, tugging the corners of Eve's mouth along with it and planting the seed of something she feared she might never fully weed out. She blinked and willed the sudden heat off her face. *Just concentrate on arranging the flowers, stupid.*

'How did you know about the small frequent meals?' he asked after a moment.

Eyes on the Queen Anne's lace she was using as a filler in one of the arrangements, Eve bit her lip. She didn't know this guy from Adam, but somehow she thought he'd understand. 'My mother. Ovarian cancer.'

'Oh. Did she ... Is she—'

Eve shook her head. 'October last year.'

'I'm so sorry.'

She glanced up to find both compassion and fear in the now slightly cloudy eucalyptus of his eyes. It propelled her to give him something to hang some hope on.

'It was detected late so the chances were never great.' *Not like your mum*, she added silently.

He gave her a shaky smile, like he'd heard her unspoken reassurance, but then sent his gaze around the shop as though searching for a change in subject. His eyes landed on the cooling cabinet behind the counter. 'Wow. What kind of flower is that?'

Eve looked over her shoulder at the stunning rose in the cabinet. 'That's a Turkish Halfeti rose. Around here, though, she's known as the onyx rose.'

Brows drawing together, he leaned on the counter. 'Why lock her up?'

'Because she fery special,' came Miriam's voice from the cool room. The older lady walked over to the cooling cabinet and gazed at the near-black rose as though it were a child she'd raised with her very own hands. Which, in a way, she had.

'Miriam travels home to her village of Halfeti every year to import the soil for the roses. They'll only bloom a near-black if planted in Halfeti soil,' Eve explained. 'People have tried growing them elsewhere, but they end up being a regular old red each and every time.'

'That is special.'

'And expensive,' Eve said. 'That's why there's only one on display. Miriam cultivates the rest in a hothouse out back.'

'How much are they?'

'One hundred dollar,' Miriam said.

'For a dozen?'

Miriam *tsk-tsked*. 'For one. But she worth it. She heal old hurts and make clear path for new love. Nice young man buy only for *fery* special lady.' Miriam winked at Eve, who rolled her eyes again.

But when Eve handed their customer his two bunches of flowers, she was sure she'd seen the smoky haze of speculation in his eyes.

~ * ~

Seven days later, Eve found her gaze snapping to the shop's door as soon as its old hinges announced the arrival of a customer. When day seven ended and the eighth one began without further sign of scotch-and-Coke hair guy, Eve convinced Miriam she needed to spend some time working in the cool room. Maybe some cold, earthy air would douse her with some much-needed sense. What had she been thinking? Nice guys who bought flowers for their mums and baby sisters were too good to be true.

Miriam allowed Eve her icy refuge until the shop phone rang. 'Is for you.' The older woman handed her the receiver and turned back to the customer she'd been serving.

'Hello, Eve speaking.'

'Eve, hi. It's Finn. You might remember I've been in a couple of times to buy flowers for my mum?'

Finn. She shouldn't decide if it was his name or the sound of his voice that sent warm toffee spreading across her chest. 'Yes, I remember.' She'd have to be in a coma to forget.

'I was planning to come in yesterday, but this latest round of chemo has hit Mum worse than the others and I don't want to leave her. I was wondering if I could have her bunch of flowers delivered? The address here is thirty-seven Laxdale Drive, Riverview.'

'I'm so sorry to hear that.' Sorry about his mother's rough round of chemo, but also that he wanted the flowers delivered because, 'I'm afraid we don't do deliveries.'

'Oh.' That one lonely word floated down the phone line wrapped in so much disappointment. 'I guess I'll come in when Mum's feeling better then.'

'I guess so. I'm so sorry I can't help, Finn.' But she could help. If she chose to she could step out from behind her worktable and bring a little happiness to a sick woman's day— and maybe earn a smile from her son. As soon as she said goodbye to Finn, Eve returned to the cool room in search of the biggest and brightest sunflowers.

~ * ~

The next time Finn walked into the store was only five days later. Not that Eve was counting or anything.

Oh please! You were so counting.

Okay, maybe she *had* been counting—because she'd made up her mind. Or Miriam had worn her down. Either way, Eve was going to ask Finn if he'd like to grab a bite to eat and maybe see a movie. Seeing the gentle way he cared for his mother, even if only for the five minutes it took to meet the fragile woman and place her flower arrangement on her dining room table, stirred a yearning for a piece of the guy's attention. No dancing though, no matter how much Meddling Miriam tried to convince her otherwise.

'Hi,' Finn said with a smile that'd found its way into Eve's daydreams.

'How's your mum doing?'

'Much better, thanks.' He rested a jeans-clad hip against the counter. No fitted T-shirt today, but the casual cotton collared shirt he wore had her itching to run her hands across his chest. To smooth out the creases, of course.

'That tea you brought really helped settle her stomach.'

A mix of something sweet yet sad pulled Eve's lips into a smile. Ginger tea had been her mother's saving grace on the really bad days. 'I'm glad she liked it.'

'She did. Almost as much as your beautiful flowers,' Finn said, and asked for the same sunflower, tulip, and peony arrangement she'd put together previously for him. Eve went about gathering the necessary items.

'My sister loved the foxtail lilies by the way.'

'Good to hear. I'm sure she'll be out with some nice guy in no time.' Speaking of which … *ask him already!*

Eve took a steadying breath, lifted her gaze to his and—

'I'd also like to buy one onyx rose today,' he said.

Eve blinked at him while the implication of his words sunk in like a clump of wet soil into plush new carpet. *So there's a girlfriend after all.*

Shoulders sinking, she pulled a long, thin cardboard box from beneath the counter. 'Special occasion?' Eve was pleased her voice didn't betray the overwhelming disappointment she felt at that moment.

'Yeah. There's someone I've been working up the courage to ask something.' He slid his hands into the pockets of his jeans and rocked on the heels of his feet. 'I'm hoping the onyx rose will convince her to say yes.'

Eve nodded and turned to the cooling cabinet, thankful he couldn't see her face for the few moments it took to lift the Halfeti rose from its bed. All this time, there'd been a girlfriend, maybe soon to become a fiancée … Eve shook her head. *Get a grip. This just proves it—no nice guys for you.*

'It'd be hard not to say yes after receiving one of these,' she said as she carefully placed the rose in the box.

'Would you?'

'Would I what?'

'Say yes.'

If a guy like Finn bought her a Halfeti rose, she'd be saying yes before the ribbon had come off the box. But she didn't tell him that. Instead, she cleared her throat and went to close the cardboard lid. 'Depends on the guy, I guess.'

A large hand stilled her smaller one. 'What about this guy?'

Eve looked up and fell into smoky eucalyptus. 'You?'

He nodded and reached into the box. 'I was told this flower should be given to someone special.' He held out the black bloom for her to take. 'Would you like to grab a bite to eat with me and maybe catch a movie?'

Eyes locked, they stood there in the flower-scented silence—because Eve had all but swallowed her tongue.

Then a voice boomed from the cool room, 'Evet! Evet de!'

Finn frowned. 'What did she say?'

Even though Miriam couldn't see her, Eve rolled her eyes. 'She said, "say yes."'

The corners of Finn's mouth twitched. 'And? What do you say?'

Eve brought the onyx rose to her face and inhaled its sweet, heady scent. There really was only one thing to do, even though she'd never hear the end of it from Miriam.

She pointed at the flamingo flower sitting to the side of the counter. 'What do you call that long yellow thing sticking out in the middle?'

Finn's brows pinched. 'You mean the stamen?'

Eve bit her lip. 'I say yes.'

Because maybe, just maybe, Eve had scored herself a nice guy after all.

A Stop-off in Noosa
By
Jillian Jones

'Maybe you could fly down … have Christmas in Melbourne with him?' My sister spoke softly, rubbing my shoulder supportively as she eyed me over the rim of her wine glass.

I sighed, brushing her arm away. 'Sarah, I've told you a thousand times, it was just a fling.'

And there he was.

My breath caught and the hubbub of chatter, laughter and music momentarily dissolved as he slipped into the seat across the table from me and his sparkling blue eyes met mine.

'Hey there.' He smiled. My heart sank. Was he that pleased to be continuing his journey? So keen to move on?

'Hi.' I felt like crap. It was our last night together and I hadn't seen him in a week. He was fresh off a flight from a six-day surfing adventure in Bali. We'd communicated via text, solely to organise his farewell.

'We need to talk. Can I steal you away for a minute?' he asked, leaning in. I nodded, but just as we stood Jen's voice reverberated down the table.

'Wait! Before you and Grace disappear, we'd like to present you with a memento of your stop-off in Noosa. A parting gift to remember us by.' Jen, my neighbour and world-class photographer, stood and walked around the table, kissing his cheek as she placed a bottle of beer and a photo album on the table in front of him. An iconic photo of Noosa beach at sunset adorned the cover.

'Thanks.' He acknowledged the beer and album with a nod

as we slid back into our seats. Our conversation would have to wait.

I'd suggested the gift idea but Jen had created it; she had all the equipment to put it together quickly and easily.

He'd merged effortlessly into my work and social circles; everyone loved him. The sixteen people gathered at the table to bid him farewell had contributed to the album. It included his favourite images of our escapades in and around the Sunshine Coast, photos from social gatherings and him out on the water. Plus, a few weeks back I'd hired Jen to do a promotional shoot for my restaurant. He'd been waiting tables the day of the shoot and, given he looked like he'd stepped from the pages of a fashion magazine, Jen convinced him to help out. She'd added those photos to the collection as well.

He flicked through the pages, tears in his eyes, but he was smiling. I knew he'd love it.

His time in Noosa had left its mark. He was infinitely hotter, his skin now perfectly tanned. His blonde hair, longer and lighter, kissed by the sun and the sea, had golden highlights through it. And he was more ripped then he'd been when he stepped off the bus that day.

My mind floated back to the moment we met …

~ * ~

'I feel bad leaving you.' Sarah handed her luggage to the bus driver.

'Stop worrying about me. I'll be fine.' I wrapped my arms around her, giving her one last hug.

'I'll text when I get home.'

I nodded. 'Now, go!' I waved her away but not before a heaviness hit my heart. She turned and stepped into the bus that would take her back home to Brisbane. My little sister had been a lifesaver, putting her own life on hold for two weeks to help me out.

I spun on my heel, about to walk away, blinking tears.

'Excuse me,' a deep, resonating male voice called from behind.

I turned. A vision in singlet top and board shorts, tall and fit with honey blonde hair. His sparkling ocean blue eyes penetrated mine. His smile was like the sun breaking through clouds on an overcast day, taking my breath away as it lifted my heavy heart. 'Are you a local?'

Tongue-tied, I nodded.

'Do you know where the tourist office is?'

I pointed to my left. It was impossible to miss the big Information sign ten steps from where we stood.

'Not sure how I missed that.' He laughed, making me laugh for the first time in weeks. There was a relaxed sense of ease and wellbeing about him.

'Can I help you with anything else?'

'Yeah. Can you recommend a good cafe? I'm starving.'

'Sure. I own the organic raw food restaurant just around the corner.'

'Must be my lucky day.' His grin said it all. 'Jacob Henderson, but call me Jake.'

'Grace.' I offered my hand. 'How long are you in Noosa?'

'Two nights, I'm heading south.' He shook my hand. 'I've just been whale watching in Hervey Bay.'

'Come on.' I smiled and waved my hand for him to follow me. 'Lunch is on me.'

~ * ~

'So why Onyx?' He'd just devoured a pumpkin and lentil salad and was licking his luscious lips as he pointed to the name of my restaurant, written in fancy script on the wall in front of him.

'It's a family name. My mother's maternal grandfather was Henry Onyx. He immigrated to Australia.'

'So nothing to do with the gem onyx?' He toyed with a black and silver ring on the ring finger of his right hand.

'No, I just liked the sound of it. Is that a black onyx?'

He nodded, removing the ring and handing it to me.

It was inscribed. This too shall pass.

'It's from my sister, Anna. She gave it to me just before I left Melbourne. It's meant to protect the wearer and also help with negative energies, including grief.'

'Why? Is she superstitious?'

'No.' He laughed. 'She's into crystals and woo-woo stuff and we had a shitty year.' His smile dropped. 'Our father died of cancer earlier this year.'

'I'm sorry to hear that.'

He shrugged. 'My brother and sister and I did nightly shifts to sit with him for twelve months before he died so we had time to say goodbye.'

'That's a tough gig,' I sympathised. I'd watched a good friend do the same last year.

He smiled. 'Thanks.' His eyes were glazed. 'My fiancée, Emma, didn't appreciate it so she ended our five-year relationship halfway through, accusing me of being more committed to work and my family than to her.'

'That's crappy,' I said as my heart went out to him. A non-committal boyfriend was the story of my life.

'I should have guessed Emma was looking for an out. She'd accepted my marriage proposal easily enough, but for two years she'd skirted around setting a wedding date,' he sighed. 'Anyway, when Dad died I decided life was too short and quit my job. I'm travelling around Australia on a ten month sabbatical. The plan is to be back in Melbourne in two months for Christmas with my brother and sister. Then I guess I'll get a real job and life will resume as normal.'

He was thirty-one, same as me. An IT specialist, but he offered to stay and help out with the dinner rush and did an impressive job waiting tables. After we closed the restaurant he joined my staff and me at the surf club for a drink. As the evening drew to a close he enticed me to the dance floor for a slow dance. Maybe it was alcohol induced but he was heavenly, holding me confidently. His scent was pure, sensual male. I'll never forget the words that won me over.

'You have the darkest brown eyes I've ever seen. They're beautiful. I can't stop looking into them and when I do it's like swimming in warm, melted chocolate. Such an addictive, delicious sensation.' Then he kissed me.

Talk about melted chocolate. I was toast.

'Stay at mine,' I begged against my better judgement.

'That's not my style. I'm only here two nights.'

'It's not my style either but I'll take whatever you're offering.'

His breath hitched and the next move totally decimated me.

A kiss so passionate my whole body threatened to go up in flames. Neither of us needed further convincing and he didn't end up staying at the hostel.

At breakfast the next morning he invited me to join him at Australia Zoo. The restaurant closed Mondays. I said yes. Hanging with him was fun. Easy.

The following day I joined him on the beach, after a no-show interview for the barista position. I wasn't having any luck finding a new staff member. Jake was meant to be catching the late bus to Brisbane, but I offered him a job for a week. He said yes and kept saying yes each week for six weeks.

The only criteria he had about working while travelling was he wouldn't do anything IT-related. However, he couldn't help himself when he found out I was having networking troubles. He fixed all the issues with the two restaurants I'd set up on the Sunshine Coast and the one I was about to open in Brisbane, plus he created a custom program to better suit my purchasing and other accounting needs. I had no idea how to repay him because he refused cash. He said I'd already paid him by offering him work, a place to stay, an awesome group of ready-made friends—and my hot body to play with.

Considerate, attentive and passionate in bed, he did wonders for my ego. I'd felt inadequate after my boyfriend of two years cheated on me with one of my table attendants—a buxom, leggy nineteen year old, blonde with fairy floss for brains. I'd come home early one evening and found them in bed together. I lost my flatmate, the boyfriend I thought was the love of my life and a good staff member in one night. I was devastated. My sister was a shoulder to cry on and a helping hand in the restaurant for two weeks, but when Jake appeared he fixed everything.

Thankfully, the day he left for Bali, a well-trained barista from Brisbane walked into the restaurant. Looking for a sea change, she'd been happy to start immediately. The empty, aching space in my heart would not be filled quite so effortlessly.

~ * ~

'I can't believe you two got me to pose like this.' Jake chuckled, pulling me from my reverie.

He lifted the album, showing me. It was the one of him wearing a waiter's uniform, holding a dish of aesthetically beautiful food in one hand and a glass of wine in the other, Onyx clearly displayed on the wall behind him. Jen had suggested he think of the best sex he'd ever had. It worked. He was swoon worthy—as enticing as the food and wine he held in his hands, inviting patrons to my restaurant.

'I thought of you.' He winked as he whispered across the table. His grin momentarily made me forget we were in a noisy, crowded bar. I took a sip of wine, hoping to quell the heat he'd generated, as he placed the album back down.

He laughed as he turned the next page.

'This has to be my all-time favourite.' Jake beamed, lifting the album again.

A photo of us kissing.

We'd just finished up the photo shoot with Jen and Jake had announced he was going surfing before the dinner rush. The restaurant was busy but I couldn't resist playfully offering him my cheek for a chaste goodbye kiss. Jake brushed across my cheek and found my lips, presenting me with a heart-stopping kiss that melted my brain and sent me weak at the knees. Jen captured it. Passion oozed from the image. I groaned as every cell of my body recalled the sensation he'd created. Heat intensified in my face and neck. Dammit. I was blushing.

'It's my favourite, too.'

He chuckled, closing the album, handing it across the table to Sarah, who'd indicated she wanted to see it.

'Thanks, everyone. It's incredible.' He raised his beer, smiling at everyone in turn.

'Cheers and good luck with choosing two from that lot.' Jen laughed and held up her wine glass.

A few weeks back Jake showed Jen and me his magnet collection. He'd purchased two souvenir magnets at each of his stopovers. Once he got back to Melbourne he planned to select two photos from each of his destinations and attach them to a magnetic board, like a travel photo collage.

Jen took a sip of her wine. 'I'd never be able to limit a travel collage to just two pictures per location.'

'No. I might have to rethink Noosa.' He tapped his beer

against my wine glass. 'Cheers!' His smile would melt icebergs. How the hell was he so happy?

The ring from his sister caught my eye. The black wave, set in silver, sat nicely on his tanned skin.

It reminded me of the inky black ocean and the nights we'd spent sitting on the beach. Magic moments I'll never forget.

I bit my bottom lip, fighting back tears I didn't want him to see. I loved those evenings with Jake. We'd wander down to the beach near my apartment after we closed the restaurant each night, sometimes with a glass of wine in hand, and sit and chat. We'd dream up new menu and marketing ideas for the restaurant and generally solve the problems of the world. It was easy, wrapped in his arms. I wanted it to last forever. Not that I'd dare mention that. When he arrived in Noosa seven weeks ago, we'd agreed this was a temporary arrangement. From my point of view he was my summer fling to get over Tom. Except I'd briefly forgotten that a week ago, the night before Jake announced he was leaving. For some reason that evening I felt so nurtured and appreciated as we sat on the beach, his arms around me. I was intoxicated, swept away by the moment, by him. Then, when he kissed me, and the kiss was so deep it touched my soul, the words came from nowhere and fell from my stupid mouth.

'I love you.'

The shocked look on his face indicated certain death. I backpedalled, laughed, said I was kidding. He remained silent– not seeing the funny side. It was fatal. Yet that night he made love to me like his life depended on it.

The next morning, however, as he packed to go away for his planned surfing trip, he uttered the words that shattered my heart.

'It's time for me to go. I can't impose on you any longer.'

I had no right to ask him to stay, and tonight was his last night. Tomorrow he'd catch a lift to Brisbane with me and continue south.

If I could see my heart right now it would look as black as the onyx on his finger. I momentarily wished my sister would buy me a black onyx ring—my grief was overwhelming.

He makes me laugh. He's a perfect balance of fun and

responsibility. I feel listened to, supported and cared for. Plus he's a damn hot lover—and he's about to walk out of my life. But he'd never promised more and his words and the look in his eyes that night confirmed he wasn't ready to commit again.

'A penny for your thoughts!' Jake pulled me back to the room.

Words wouldn't come.

'Dance with me?' He stood, offering his hand as a slow song filled the air. He led me to the dance floor.

'I connected with a couple of IT guys from here on my surfing trip.' His cheek on mine, holding me close, wrapping me in his familiar masculine scent.

'Really? Who'd have thought the Sunny Coast was a haven for surfing IT-nerds?' I teased. He laughed.

'I've accepted a job with them.'

My brain seized up. I couldn't process his words.

He licked his lips, looking nervous. 'It's for three months, initially. One project. But if I get it right they'll offer me a partnership. They've got work coming out of every orifice.'

He stopped and waited, looking like a hopeful puppy.

'What about your plans? Am I dropping you off in Brisbane tomorrow?'

'I'll go with you tomorrow to replace the modem and add a switch—'

'Aren't you finishing your trip?' I interrupted.

He cleared his throat and scratched his head. 'I changed my mind.'

My thoughts smashed in on each other like a wave crashing against the shoreline. 'I don't understand.' Was I hearing right? I didn't want to get my hopes up.

'Grace, you surprised me that night. I thought we were on the same page, but when you said you loved me, the words made my heart sing. Except it didn't sit right with the short-term thing. I got confused … panicked.' He pulled away slightly and we stood there.

They say the eyes are the windows to the soul. Maybe it's true, because his gaze penetrated so deep I was sure he was reading my mind, seeing all my secrets. I felt weak. Vulnerable.

'When Emma left me, I vowed never to give my heart away

again, but this last week, with space and time to think, to get clarity, I realised I don't want a life without you. I phoned my brother and sister today. Told them I met this woman.' He grinned. 'She's beautiful, intelligent, nurturing and inspiring.' His fingers brushed my cheek. 'And I've fallen madly in love with her.'

My heart thumped against my chest as I caught my breath.

His smile was brighter than the full moon glowing through the window behind him.

'Don't you want to be home for Christmas?'

'I'll go if you come with me. Just for Christmas. I want you to meet my brother and sister but I'm planning on staying right here in Noosa with you.'

His words were like a relieving and rejuvenating breeze on a hot summer's day as he pulled me closer.

'I'd like that.' I smiled and kissed him.

Heart of Stone
By
Fiona Marsden

'Black is the colour of my true love's heart.'

Augusta Whitcombe savoured the words, running the tip of her tongue over her lips, chapped from the wind funnelling along the London street outside.

Lord Evan Blackleith, like many men before him, had proved himself to have naught but a stone where his heart should beat. A heart as black and hard as the onyx panels adorning the Italian Salon at Castle Blackleith.

'Miss Whitcombe?' How was it that such a cold man should have a voice warm enough to melt the snows of a bleak midwinter?

She turned slowly, bracing herself for the jolt that came each time her eyes rested on Evan's compelling, saturnine countenance. It struck her as always, mid-chest, a sharp pain stealing her breath followed by an ache behind her ribs. A dark shadowy presence, he stood at the open door of the salon, the narrow, hard boned face topped by silky black hair, carelessly brushed back from an intellectual brow.

She dipped her head in acknowledgment. 'Lord Blackleith.'

'What brings you here on such a foul day, Miss Whitcombe? I swear a fall of snow would be far better than this bitter frost and treacherous wind.'

She glanced beyond him at the footman hovering in the hall. 'I wish to speak to you. Privately.'

He shut the door and sauntered across to the ornate, black marble fireplace, removing his gloves and tossing them onto a matching marble-topped side table on the way. 'I hardly think we have anything to say to each other. I'm surprised to find you here at all. Unchaperoned.' His finely drawn mouth curled at the last word.

Clutching her reticule close to her stomach as if it would steady the churning inside, Augusta forced herself to remain calm. 'Things have changed. In any case, I am over twenty-two.'

'Almost an ape-leader.' With a faint sigh, he indicated a wing chair by the fire. 'Pray be seated. I can see you will not leave without unburdening yourself.'

She perched on the edge of the chair, unnerved when he didn't move to take the opposite seat. He towered above her, far too tall, too broad in the shoulder, too everything. One arm propped against the mantle, his hair and suit blended with the marble, white neckcloth contrasting with his sun darkened skin.

'Won't you sit, Lord Blackleith?'

His eyes, a pale indeterminate colour between grey and green, framed by thick, stubby black lashes, flickered. 'Do you expect to exhaust me with your eloquence?'

She clamped her lips together as a surge of giveaway warmth flooded her skin. Only Evan could discompose her with a look from those compelling eyes.

He moved then, an impatient shrug telling of his annoyance. 'Very well. The sooner we get this over with the better.'

With him sprawled in the seat opposite her, Augusta wondered if perhaps she had been too hasty. His long legs in their tight pantaloons and Hessian boots stretched much too close to her own feet tucked primly in front of her. He was beautifully proportioned. Muscular in the way of an active man who rode, drove and visited a salon to try his skills as a pugilist. She had known his strength, intimately, once. She dismissed the past with the contempt it deserved. It was the present that counted. 'Andrew tells me he owes you something over two thousand pounds.'

'Guineas.'

~ * ~

'Guineas?'

Evan watched the colour in her face fade, leaving only two

patches of bright rouge on her cheeks. Augusta painting her face disturbed him. Her clear skin used to have all the colour it needed, a delicate creamy tint with a flush of colour on the high cheekbones and lips a soft rosy pink. Framed by her brown ringlets that never relied on papering or hot irons. Her pointed chin and masterful nose prevented any but the most charitable from calling her a beauty but something in her soft brown eyes had caught his attention even at seventeen. He'd not courted her then, or paid her more than the briefest civility. A chit barely out of the schoolroom had nothing to offer a man of his experience. Yet experience taught a man patience.

'Yes, Augusta. Two thousand guineas.'

'Surely you could have stopped him.'

'Andrew is past twenty-five years. If he chooses to lose the better part of his fortune at the tables, it is hardly my concern.'

He saw her mouth open to object, and then close.

'Exactly, Augusta. He is not my concern. Not anymore.'

'I thought you were fond of him.'

'Fond I may be. But not doting.'

She was silent for a moment, her dark eyes shadowed. 'He has not the money to pay you.'

A ball of anger uncoiled in his stomach. 'Did he send you here to beg for clemency?'

'No. He is trying to raise it in the city.'

'He'll not get anything from the cent-per-cents.'

'Will you not help him?'

'You cannot coddle him forever, Augusta.'

'He is to be married in the spring. This could ruin everything.'

'For her sake, I hope her dowry is tied up.'

If anything, she became paler.

Leaning forward, he studied her averted face. She was surely thinner and dark shadows hollowed her fine eyes. She suffered, for what reason he didn't dare guess. It had been more than six months since he'd seen her this close. Early summer. He'd left almost immediately for the continent and only returned for Christmastide at Blackleith, nearly a month past. 'Who is the girl?'

'Miss Philby. She has no fortune, only a competence.'

'Don't tell me it's love.'

Colour washed back into her face. 'There is no reason to sneer. Indeed, they are in love. It is an ideal match for she enters into all Andrew's interests.'

'His gambling?'

She bit her lip. 'We thought he had finished with the cards.'

'Perhaps he was lured in against his will. His cronies were all there that night.'

'We hope the marriage will settle him. If he remains in the country for much of the year, surely the temptations must be less.'

'Miss Philby is agreeable?'

'Yes.' A darting glance accompanied the bare word.

He sucked in a breath, tasted her clean floral scent, and regretted it. 'What of you, Augusta? Has your brother found a worthy suitor for your hand?'

~ * ~

The harsh words forced her attention to his face. Augusta stared at him, hardly believing he would be so cruel. 'I shall never marry.'

His lips twitched in a half smile. 'You surprise me.'

'I discovered I have no desire to place myself in the power of any man. Least of all a husband.' She tilted her chin at him, knowing he would see past her false defiance. Her lie.

He steepled his long elegant fingers, his gaze resting on them in sombre contemplation. A delicate gold ring set with an oval stone of polished onyx caught the light on the small finger of his left hand. She pressed her hand to her stomach to settle it. Unsuccessfully. He spoke and she forced herself to concentrate.

'I wonder what you would be prepared to give to save your brother this time.'

'Save my brother ...' A cold finger traced its way down her spine, expanding around her ribcage to chill her to the core. 'You are prepared to spare him ... in return for something?'

The pale eyes glinted, a light in them she hadn't seen for a long time. 'What are you prepared to give?'

'I have jewellery. My grandmother's pearls. Some small items, gifts.'

The chuckle had no humour. Rather it had a sinister ring. 'Trumpery, my dear girl. Even with the pearls, it wouldn't fetch two thousand guineas or anything near that amount.'

'What do you want?' She knew the answer. He sought to humiliate her. As he had done all those months ago.

His smile illuminated his grim visage. 'You, of course.'

A curl of anger twisted at the base of her throat. 'You've had me, and found me wanting.'

'Wanting? Did you think so?' His brows drew together, accentuating the crease between them.

'What else could I think when you immediately flaunted your mistress throughout the town?'

'That was most careless of me.'

The anger solidified into a cold lump, almost choking her. 'C-careless? A deliberate slight. It was deliberate, wasn't it?'

'Yes.'

'And the rumours? You set them about. As if I weren't humiliated enough.'

'I know nothing about any rumours.'

'You left town before they took hold. Still, I'm sure your mistress took great delight in telling you of the results.'

'I had no contact with anyone for some months whilst travelling.'

The frown was back, his eyes focused on her face. Her skin tingled as warmth spread under his intent stare. Curiosity won over pride. 'Where could you have been, that letters would not find you?'

'I was some months in Dalmatia and from there travelled to Constantinople. I was in Egypt when the letter about my mother's failing health reached me.'

Guilt brought a tinge of dismay. 'I should have inquired. How is your mother?'

'Better for seeing her errant son.' His wry smile poked a hole in her reserve.

'I'm glad. She is very fond of you.'

'She is also fond of you. I was told plainly of my foolishness in letting you go. I reminded her that I was the injured party. You jilted me.'

The pain flowed back unchecked. She pushed at her chest

with her fist but it did nothing to assuage the ache. 'What choice did I have? Even if you still wished to wed me, should I have married you in the face of your clear declaration of intent? I saw enough of that with my father's parade of women. He at least had some excuse.'

A dark flush mantled his cheekbones. 'I had forgotten your parents.' He shifted, his shoulders rising and falling, as if casting off a heavy weight. 'You had what you wanted. I cleared your brother's debts. It was supposed to be the last time.'

'That wasn't what I wanted. You offered. I thought you did it out of love for me. I was a fool.'

~ * ~

Evan bit back the protest pricking his tongue. Rising abruptly, he moved to lean on the back of the chair. Where he couldn't see the reproach in her eyes, taste the scent of her each time he inhaled. He'd been the fool.

'You thought I was so lost in love you could ask anything of me in my weakness and there would be no accounting? I'm not so easily manipulated.'

'You are the master manipulator, Evan. I thought you intended to marry me. I believed everything you said to me. The endearments, the protectiveness.'

He could feel himself stiffen. 'I intended to marry you.'

She stood to confront him, sidestepping the chair between them. 'After you had already taken what you wanted? A Blackleith, taking a despoiled bride to the altar? I don't think so.' Shock froze him for a moment as Augusta returned his look with a haughty lift of her nose. 'This is pointless. I'll leave you to gloat at the downfall of my family.' She made for the door.

'Wait. Will you be at the Palmerston's ball?'

Her eyes flashed before she lowered her lashes demurely. 'I was not invited.'

There was something here he did not understand. 'Why not?'

'Ruined women do not attend soirees.' There was a conviction in her tone that disturbed. Had he done so much damage? Even if it were well deserved, it sat uncomfortably in his gut.

'Does your money support your brother's gambling?'

She snorted, a small snuffly sound he'd always found endearing when they were courting. 'He retains enough honour not to ask.' She tilted her head. 'I will give him what I have, all the same.'

'You won't have to. I'll forgive his debt.'

Her sharp upwards glance held something like pain. 'In return for what.'

'If we resume where we left off.' At least the ache in his loins would be assuaged. He'd not needed any woman while he travelled yet the moment he arrived back in England, began to think about seeing Augusta, his body had come to life.

'You surely don't wish to resume our betrothal?'

The doubtful tone and raised brows told him she had no illusions. 'Our relationship will be discreet, but informal.'

Her mouth opened and closed, a ruddy flush suffusing the pale skin. 'You want me to be your mistress?'

His stomach rebelled at the sordid description. 'Lover. We will be lovers.'

Her spurt of laughter caught him on the raw, his skin itching under the fine linen. He clenched his fists, holding them rigid at his side, else he would reach out to her. Touch her. Perhaps strangle her. Maybe then the pain in his heart would go away.

'Lovers?' She spat the word in between the almost hysterical peels of sound. Finally, she drew herself up, dabbing at her face with an edge of a sleeve. 'We were never lovers. Lovers are supposed to be in love.' She shook her head. 'There is no love between us, Evan. I doubt if there ever was.'

The pain spiked as he recalled the desolation of discovering that inevitable truth. He'd left her before dawn in the heights, but his return mid-morning had plunged him into the depths. 'I know. I learned it when I returned to your brother's house and heard you talking to Lady Addison.'

~ * ~

He'd heard her talking to Letty Addison? Augusta frowned. 'She is the worst gossip in London. Do you think I would tell her anything of importance? It would be all over town in a day.'

'I heard you telling her of your triumph. Of catching a man wealthy enough to support you and your brother in the first style.'

'You think I should have spoken of love to a woman who married a man old enough to be her father for his wealth and position?'

'Was there a difference between your ambitions?'

She could hardly breathe for the rage burning in her chest. 'My ambition does not include being your mistress. I've been your mistress before, Lord Blackleith. It brought me nothing but pain and humiliation.'

'You were not my mistress. We were to be married.'

'Were we? Most of my acquaintances seemed doubtful once they knew of my indiscretion. All my supposed friends suddenly realised that my presence was not required at their parties and dinners. I was given the cut direct by half of London when I attended the theatre.'

He stood quite still, staring at her, his dark brows drawn together. 'I told no one. Not even my brother. At least he … Cedric may have guessed.'

'You told your mistress. That was enough.'

'I had no mistress. Have no mistress.'

'So, who was the high-flyer you flaunted down James Street that very afternoon?'

'My brother's ladybird. He loaned her for an hour or two.'

Nausea tightened her throat. 'You took her to bed that same day?'

'Of course not. All I intended was to punish you a little. I didn't think you would refuse to marry me because of it.'

'Why would you think I would accept a marriage contract with a man who flaunted a fancy piece as a declaration that he intended to keep a mistress after his wedding?'

His long fingers dug furrows through the thick black locks. With his bottom lip tucked under his teeth he looked almost vulnerable. His shoulders dipped and rose in a shrug. 'Because you wanted the money.'

So that was what he thought of her. She straightened her back and looked him directly in the eyes. 'Not enough to live with a rake for a husband. I grew up watching my mother ignore the pity and sly comments because of my father's indiscretions. It is not my idea of a successful match.'

'Are you saying you loved me?'

'I loved who I thought you were. It is not the first time a woman has mistaken a man's character.'

'A man's character is not something you can mistake. We know each other well enough not to fall into error on that point.'

Augusta snorted. 'Yet here we are. You believing I am willing to become your mistress. I do not think I mistook your character.'

She stepped back as he crossed the room with his long stride. He stopped, so close. The scent of leather and his own distinctive aroma caught in her throat. A long finger tilted up her chin, warmth radiating from the point of contact. His mouth softened.

'What are we doing to each other, my Aggie?'

The affectionate diminutive brought tears to her eyes. 'I don't know. It all happened so quickly. Is it possible to love truly in only a few weeks?'

'The love was true. For trust, we needed more time. I am not your father, sweetling.'

'It seemed you were for that one day.'

His eyes darkened. 'I was a fool. In my heart, I knew you loved me. Why else did you give yourself so freely?'

'We were both foolish.'

He took her hand and she watched in wonder as he slid the onyx ring onto her finger. 'Marry me, my love?'

'I am a fallen woman, you must know.'

His smile spoke of tenderness and regret. 'It is my duty to restore your honour, and mine.'

The cold lump in her chest warmed at last. 'I accept.'

Warm lips brushed hers, lighting a flame under the skin. His palm rested lightly upon her breast. 'You have carried my heart all these months.'

'I have felt it.' She lay her hand on his, pressing it against her chest.

'A burden?' His voice was soft.

'Heavy as stone.'

'Together the load will be lighter.'

Already it soared. He must surely feel it flutter under his

touch. 'Together sounds like heaven.'

Strong arms wrapped her around. 'Paradise.'

Beneath the Waves
By
Stella Quinn

The water was cool down here in the deep. Cooler than she had anticipated. Silver glimmered from passing shoals of fish and shadows flickered, here in the quiet waters of the Pacific.

Sally paused at the strip of red fabric tied about the heavy rope; she'd reached the sixty-foot mark. Twenty feet below her was the *Antoinette*. She peered into the darkness. Nothing loomed. Leaving one gloved hand skimming over the tough fibres of the rope, she resumed her even pace, her dive fins propelling her steadily downwards. One foot per second; she knew the rules. No one who worked in ship salvage could afford to break them. Bad decisions this far underwater cost lives. She should know, she thought grimly. Her father had died on a salvage dive.

She sucked in a breath as the ancient black wreck of the *Antoinette* came into view, her bubbles curling away like quicksilver as she exhaled. No matter that she'd seen it two dozen times or more by now. It was majestic. And more than a little spooky. She checked her watch, its oversized digits gleaming in the light of her head torch. 3.02 pm. She was late.

Sally took a moment to watch the particles of debris the ocean was pushing by, judging the current, before finning her way along the starboard beam of the ship. Colin would be cranky if she kept him waiting much longer. Cranky and cold. A thirty-minute shift at eighty feet was tough even for old sea dogs like him.

The flurry of sand kicked up by the pump came into view

before he did. She swam up beside him, tugging on his flipper to get his attention. He looked up from the section of wreck he was working on and made an "o" with his fingers. She signalled okay in return, gave him a fist pump and a wave, and swam in beside him to swap places on the pump. Her shift had begun.

~ * ~

Pete slid the muslin-bound journal into its dry sack and peered past the dock and out to sea. Where were they? He checked the screen of his phone for the third time and swore. No reception. He was ready to give his secretary a blast, to hell with the time difference. He wondered if he'd made a mistake letting the taxi driver leave. If you could call it a taxi. The passenger seats had been covered with leopard-print vinyl, which only partly distracted him from the holes in the carpeted footwell, through which dust from the unsealed road had smothered him for the ninety-minute drive from Savusavu airport on the island of Vanua Levu.

He pulled at the damp collar of his shirt. The sun was barely up and he was roasting. And jet-lagged. Fiji in late December was going to take some getting used to after snowbound New York. Still. It would be worth it if the reports from the salvage operators were true. His museum had been searching for news of the lost Bell-Allen treasure for years. He was just more used to conducting his searches and acquisitions in the plush high-rises of cities. Where there were chairs. Climate-controlled air-conditioning. And where the people he met with were on time.

A throaty engine noise pulled him out of his daydream of cool air and comfort and he looked up. A dinghy was speeding its way towards the concrete dock. He smiled, amused by the incongruity of his surroundings. It was a hell of a way to start negotiations for an acquisition.

~ * ~

Sally pulled in to the dock, muttering to herself, as she had been for the twenty-minute ride from her salvage boat. How in hell Colin had talked her into getting some city-slick expert to verify their findings, she was having trouble remembering. It must have been oxygen deficiency. Or rum. If there was one thing she had no patience for, it was armchair experts.

Throwing a rope over a stalk of rusted steel, she used her other hand to cut the motor and turned to take stock of Colin's expert. Well. She hadn't expected cute. Standing on the dock, looking rumpled and tired and just a bit cranky, stood six foot of handsome male. She frowned up at him.

'Peter Churchill?'

'Yep.'

Sally took a moment to drink him in. Dark hair. It was cut short—ruthlessly so, but the hint of a curl remained. A dark shadow framed his jawline. She couldn't decide whether he was in need of a shave or following fashion. Brown eyes stared down at her and the eyebrows above gave a quirk.

'So do I jump aboard?'

She realised she'd been staring and cleared her throat. 'Sure. Chuck your bags down. Driest place is up front.'

He dropped down into the dinghy and tucked his canvas duffel into the vee of the prow. He looked about uncertainly then sat on the inflated rim opposite her. 'No life jacket?' he said.

She laughed. 'Mate. Relax. It's a duck pond out there.'

'Okay,' he said. 'What about a name? You don't look much like a Colin'.

Sally pull-started the motor with a quick jerk of her arm. 'Sally,' she said as the motor roared into life. She eased it into gear. 'Unhook the rope will you, Pete? I'm Colin's business partner. The one who found the *Antoinette*.'

~ * ~

Pete leaned against the rail, feeling the boat roll over the slight swell. He'd stripped down to shorts and taken a swim off the diving platform—the relief had been immeasurable. Salt crystals had dried on his bare chest and the sea breeze had lifted, pushing cool fingers through his hair.

Sally and Colin were busy on the equipment deck. Watching them work had been eye opening. Two shifts each in the morning, then again after lunch, their schedule ruled by depths and oxygen. Sally's first shift had brought up a sack of encrusted metal, probably coins, and Colin was gearing up for his turn.

Pete watched him fit the tank over his wetsuit, the breathing apparatus lying like a black octopus over his shoulders. Colin slid into the water and Pete switched his gaze to Sally.

Her hair blazed in the sunlight, a reddish-blonde mane of curls. She was short, lean in places. She hefted a weight belt and lowered it into the freshwater bucket, giving him an unobstructed view down the front of her unzipped wetsuit. Not lean everywhere, he thought, feeling a thump of arousal as she stood and caught his gaze. He hadn't expected to be charmed by a soft-eyed, tough-talking salvage operator who might well hold the key to the treasure he had been pursuing since college. Perhaps not all the treasure to be found in the Pacific was going to be beneath the waves.

He made his way over to the work area. 'Can I give you a hand?'

She handed him the sack of salvage. 'How good are you with a scrubbing brush and acid?'

He smiled at her, deliberately making it cocky. 'I'm good at loads of things.'

~ * ~

Had he been flirting with her? Sally cleared the tools from the workbench in the saloon. She scowled to herself, remembering the flurry of heat that had run up her face as he'd murmured provocatively to her on deck. She didn't have time for a romance with some big shot from the city. She sighed. If only he didn't look so much like a pirate. Her blood was starting to run just a little hotter each time he eased past her in the confines of the boat.

'Table's clear,' she called out and walked over to the safe to bring out the salvage they had found.

This was the moment. Pete held his breath while Sally spun the combination of the safe. The Bell-Allen treasure. Could he really be about to unravel the mystery?

Sally dropped a bag onto the worktable and slapped Pete's hand away as he reached to open it. 'Not so fast, handsome. You tell me why you couldn't just give us an answer by email. What was it that had you hot-footing it all the way down here?'

'Call it an academic hunch,' he said.

'A hunch about what?' She took the mug Colin was passing

to her and set the coffee down. A chunk of grey matter floated on the surface. She poked it with a screwdriver to make it dissolve. Powdered milk took some getting used to.

Pete smiled. History and persuasion had always been his strong suits. 'When I was in college, I majored in antiquities. Particularly antiquities that had been lost then found. Salvaged, to use your term.' He winked at Colin. Sally's views on salvage and his own had been argued out non-stop since he'd come aboard. He believed treasure belonged in a museum for all to enjoy. Sally believed in the code of all salvage operators: finders keepers.

'Okay,' said Sally, hurrying him along.

'Well, based on Colin's photo, I think what you've stumbled on,' he pointed a finger to the depths below their anchored boat, 'includes pieces from the Bell-Allen treasure.'

Sally frowned. 'We haven't just stumbled on this wreck, Pete. While you've been wearing fancy suits and drinking lattes in New York, we've been researching, reading diaries, grid-searching miles of sea bed.'

Pete slid a long finger over the back of her hand, enjoying the feel of his skin on hers. 'Sorry, Sal. I didn't mean to imply you haven't worked hard to get to this moment. I just mean while you were hunting for a wreck in the hope it would contain items of value, you haven't been searching for the Bell-Allen treasure in particular.'

She shrugged. 'That's true. I've never heard of it. It certainly wasn't mentioned in any of our research.'

'The treasure was lost back in the nineteenth century. The treasure itself dates back much further than that. Parts of it, at least.'

'Spell it out for us, son,' said Colin.

'The Bell-Allens were minor nobles from England. In the height of the British rule in India, a younger son moved to Bombay, where he amassed a fortune as a merchant. He took a particular interest in jewellery and hoarded away a great collection before dying of dysentery.'

'There's a lot of Indian jewellery from that era. What made his collection so special?'

Pete smiled. 'The merchant, John, was rumoured to be

having an affair with the wife of an Indian Prince. Her husband had given her, as a wedding present, a pendant of black onyx marbled with veins of white. The pendant was said to have been in their family for so long it had been a gift from the gods.'

'And she gave it to John?' Colin said.

Pete shrugged. 'Or he stole it? That part of the mystery we don't know. We do know that the Indian Prince had his wife executed as punishment.'

Sally was hooked, despite herself. She was, after all, a treasure hunter.

'But then John died. His nephew travelled to India to bring home his effects, but there's no record of him returning to England. We know he arrived in Bombay, because we have the lawyer's records, witnessing the nephew crating up the possessions. That's where our trail ran cold. Sixteen ships set sail from Bombay in the weeks following the packing of the crates. We've researched them all through their insurance records. What we've never researched, however, is the brigantine that sailed out of Bombay three months later. A double-masted trading brig, bound for New Zealand, with a hold full of spices and silk.

Sally took a deep breath. 'The *Antoinette*.'

Pete flashed her a grin. She ignored the way it tugged at her heart and carefully emptied the bag onto the table.

A signet ring gleamed dully in the afternoon light, its gold and ruby setting thick with the grime of a century beneath the waves. Pete pulled a jeweller's scope towards him and inspected it. This was the piece Colin had photographed and emailed to him. The etching was faint, but it was there. His equipment at the museum would be able to calibrate depth and magnify the design, but his gut knew. The Bell-Allen emblem was etched into the soft gold of the ring.

He turned his attention to the other items. A brooch, the green stone undoubtedly emerald. Bracelets. Metal buttons, coins, a buckle that may have come from a shoe. No necklace. He tried not to feel the disappointment; they hadn't found it yet, but they were close.

Pete flipped open the muslin journal holding the lawyer's inventory of the Bell-Allen treasure. 'Sixteenth century diamond and emerald brooch. Hexagonal-cut emerald, gold work in floral design, thirteen diamonds forming the petals,' he read.

Colin picked up the brooch, running an oil-stained thumb over it. He grinned. 'It's an exact match.'

Pete shared a look with Sally. 'This is the first recorded sighting of an item from the Bell-Allen treasure since it was crated for shipment in 1887.'

'And the value of this brooch?' Colin pushed him.

Pete shook his head. 'I'm a museum curator. You know my opinion on this. Priceless. But of course, commercially, it has value. It's not as large as the emerald brooch created for Catherine the Great of Russia, but as a guide, hers sold at auction recently for 1.6 million.'

Sally gaped, stunned. Over one million dollars. She shot a look at Colin, her eyes suddenly wet with unshed tears. He gave her wrist a squeeze. He would know what she was feeling. Her father had given his life to marine salvage, without ever finding enough to do more than stay a few steps ahead of his creditors. It was his research that had led them to the *Antoinette*. How she wished he could have been here.

Pete patted a hand on the empty sack. 'Nothing more?'

Colin grunted. 'It doesn't just sparkle on the seabed waiting for us to pick it up, son. There's four hundred tons of disintegrated wooden boat and cargo mixed up down there. We've barely sifted five percent of the wreck.'

'I can get a team here,' said Pete. 'A second boat, more divers.' He looked at his watch. 'What time is it in New York?' he muttered to himself, and started scrabbling on the table for a pen.

Sally threw up a hand. 'Just pull on the reins a second there, Tonto,' she said. 'This is our wreck.'

Pete paused. 'You're right,' he said. 'Sorry, I got carried away. But,' he rested a hand on her arm, 'maybe we could think about a joint venture? You and Colin are credited with the find. We pool our resources—your search for the ship, my research on the Bell-Allens— and we decide together what gets sold and what gets saved?'

Sally shared a look with Colin. He knew as well as she did how down-to-the-wire their finances were. A second boat, more equipment, money and expertise to salvage the *Antoinette* properly? It was tempting. She raked her gaze over Pete. Too tempting. Could she trust him? That was the question. She wanted to. And the thought of spending more time with him, finding out if the flirty comments and steamy looks had some substance to them ... oh yes. She was tempted.

'I need to think,' she said. 'It's a big decision. There's a meke on the beach tonight at the little eco resort. A Fijian dance ceremony,' she clarified, seeing the blank look on Pete's face. 'Why don't we all go? It's not far on the dinghy. It'll give me a few hours away from the boat, so I can clear my head and think. Can you wait that long, Pete?'

Pete smiled, and her heart did a little flip-flop in her chest. 'I'm good at waiting.'

~ * ~

The figures in warpaint and grass skirts had laid down their spears and picked up electric guitars. A drumroll cut through the wet heat of the early evening. Sally smiled. *Baby It's You*, she thought, recognising the seventies rock song. No wonder she loved Fiji. The modern world had infiltrated its south seas culture without destroying it. She could feel the thrum of the drum beat pumping in her chest.

She looked across the table at Pete to see if he was enjoying the contrast as much as she was. But he wasn't watching the band. His eyes were on her. Intent. Bold. She reared her head back a fraction as the sexual heat rising off him came at her like a slap. Oh. So this was how it was going to go.

She was dimly aware of the music sliding into a looser beat; electric keyboard and deep voices, something a bit Stevie Wonder. The music added to the wave of desire. The long look from Pete was like a riptide, pulling her into deep water. She drained the ice in her glass and set it back on the table.

'Okay,' she said.

Pete smiled. For an office boy from the city, he had the smile of a buccaneer. 'Okay, we're starting a joint venture?' he asked.

She pulled him to his feet. 'That's not all we're starting,' she said. She had to lean in close to be heard over the band. 'Back to the boat,' she said. 'Right now. You and me.' And then she bit him lightly on the neck. Just because his skin was right there. Just because she could. She leaned back and her eyes met his, their deep brown running into black, hot as pitch, like onyx in a fire. It was going to be a fast ride back to the boat, she thought, her mind already feeling the throttle rip open under her hand. She was just in the mood for a wild ride with a pirate.

Hope
By
Frances Dall'Alba

Abby ached all over, her neck twisted uncomfortably on the sand. Granules covered her face and filled her mouth. She spat, trying to remove the knotted strands of her dark shoulder-length hair caught in her mouth. Slowly opening her eyes, she saw the pale dawn stretched across the sky. A cool breeze licked along her bare arms and legs. She still wore the cotton shorts and shirt she had worn to bed.

She tried to move her left leg. Alarm shot through her. She couldn't feel it. Then memories of what happened exploded behind her eyes and she burst into tears.

Something moved beside her and she heard a hoarse, 'Are you okay?'

Panic shot through her as she attempted to roll over. She grimaced, pain arching along her back. A man lay on her leg. A gash along his right cheek was congealed with blood, his rustic-brown hair matted and clumped in disarray.

'I ... I can't feel my leg.'

Noises began to emerge and filled the blank spaces of her head. All of a sudden she heard cries for help, planes flying overhead and frantic voices directing and ordering. Had she really not heard anything moments earlier?

Out of the chaos around them, the man began to chuckle. 'I'm sorry. That's me on your leg. No wonder you can't feel much.' Shifting away, his hand reached down and uncrossed their legs, starting a rush of blood back into her leg.

'Is that any better?'

She tried to nod. Letting her face fall back onto the sand, the tears started again. Where was her sister? What about Zoe? The cruise was supposed to be the holiday of a lifetime, encompassing Antarctica and South America. They had been a day away from docking in Rio, their last port.

The previous night they had danced and drunk a little too much. Making their way to their room, swaying arm in arm, they had sung pieces of everything they knew, making their own music.

The first explosion happened in the small hours of the morning. Alarms sounded and life jackets were shoved at them. The fire spread quicker than word could. On the deck, with the lifeboats full, they were told to jump overboard and swim for the coast, several kilometres away.

In the black of night, she had lost her sister and Zoe. The only light was coming from the inferno of fire quickly taking over the ship. With each new explosion, she heard more shouting, more terrified voices.

Hours later, despair clutching at her chest, her voice was hoarse from shouting their names over and over, to no avail. The waves relentlessly pounded at her paltry efforts to swim, her arms tiring quickly. When the ache became too much and her voice no longer carried sound, she lay on her back, letting the life jacket keep her afloat and the current to take her at its will.

~ * ~

'Oh my God,' the man exclaimed.

Her eyes snapped open. She struggled to sit up.

'Here, let me.'

He helped her into a sitting position and supported her, resting her back against his chest. Her mouth dropped at the carnage spread across the isolated beach. In the distance, the large cruise ship was still burning, slowly sinking, passengers still clinging to the exposed deck.

Bodies lay strewn along the beach for two hundred metres. Some moved, most didn't. Lifeless bodies bobbed in the water, reaching the beach with each wave and then being dragged out to sea again when the wave withdrew. Overhead, parachutists dropped from planes.

She gasped, standing with a rush. 'I have to find my sister and Zoe. Oh my God, I ...'

She fell, unable to stand on her leg.

He swiftly got on his feet and picked her up, holding her in his strong arms. 'I'll help you. Were you travelling with anyone else?'

She shook her head. 'What about you?' Her voice came out gravelly, the crunch of sand between her teeth sounding loud.

'Two mates. They were still partying when I decided to call it a night. God help them, they could have been anywhere when this happened.'

Eyes glued to the scene, they witnessed boats continuing to arrive. Some collected bodies from the water, some rescued those clinging to the ship, others came to shore with medical assistance.

Hobbling, her left leg still in pain, she agreed to his suggestion to get out of the sun. She knew they wouldn't be a priority compared to the injured needing immediate attention.

She was alive. She could process that much.

She let him lead her away. Looking up, tropical forests covered numerous peaks, running along the length of the small patch of exposed beach. She knew they were a day south of Rio. A hundred kilometres north or south and they would have landed on a populated beach. Help would have come immediately. Instead, they had beached on impenetrable country, the reason why supplies had to be shipped in or dropped from above. It was too much for her troubled mind to deal with. Not until she knew if her sister and friend were alive.

She leaned heavily on his arm, the shade a welcome relief.

'Can you make it to those smooth rocks over there? We can sit for a minute.'

She nodded, glad she didn't have to think past the basics. As they got closer, she spotted water trickling down vertical rocks. She pointed and he understood immediately. He helped her over the slippery and moss-covered rocks, until they stood beneath the small stream of water. She was grateful for anything and held her face up against it. The water trickled over her hair, her eyes and her open mouth, every drop finding a home.

The relief was instant.

He did the same.

'Careful. You have a cut.' Reaching up, she touched it, his stubble scratching against her soft skin. 'It's not too bad.'

Gingerly fingering it, he nodded. 'I can't remember when that happened.'

She made to sit down, this perfect little Eden unexpectedly calming her, when she knew she had no right to. Would she find her sister and friend alive?

He sat beside her, his fingers prodding at the pebbles and rocks near his foot.

'I'm not surprised you're an Aussie. There seemed to be more of us than anyone else on board.'

She allowed herself a sad smile. It had been a great cruise. They had met so many new people.

'Hey, look at this.'

She turned and watched as he polished a smooth, black rock with his thumb. It sat neatly in the palm of his hand, his fingers rolling it from side to side. 'My grandfather is a bit of a gem enthusiast. I should take it back to him.'

She noticed another near his other foot and picked it up. 'Here's another one.'

He went to take it but stopped. 'How about you keep it? Treat it like a good luck charm. We might both need it.'

She squeezed her hand around it, knowing what he meant. Hidden in this private alcove, she inhaled a lungful of the forest's freshness and held onto to it for as long as she could. She would do anything to invigorate her soul before her mind disallowed it. She shouldn't be at peace yet. Find the others first, then enjoy it.

Stumbling up, she said, 'I need to go back. Find out what I can. Will you help me walk?'

'Of course. By the way, I'm Mark.'

'I'm Abby. Thanks for your help.'

'I may need yours soon. Keep a tight hold on that rock.'

~ * ~

Panic set the mood for the day as it progressed. Uninjured passengers found themselves helping the medics, accomplishing the impossible and yet no match for the number of bodies still washing up along the shore. By midday, injured passengers took the first boats back to the closest hospitals. The white-shrouded bodies next. The uninjured waited their turn. Lists of names were compiled, details and photos taken, faces searched. Abby did not find the faces she so desperately wanted to.

By the time the afternoon sun had washed along the shore, causing the leaves to droop from its intensity, Mark's confidence had wilted, too. There was no sign of his mates either.

They were told by officials the boats would continue to work the night shift, moving the deceased bodies before the next day's heat set in. Those left behind were given food and told to take a blanket each.

With flagging spirits, Mark picked up two blankets and two bottles of water, while she reached for some of the food on offer. Taking an extra helping for Mark, she didn't think she could eat much that night.

Mark carried a torch and she followed with her head down, her feet following his footsteps in the sand. When he stopped, she walked into him. 'Sorry.'

He dropped the blankets to the sand. 'Leave the food here. We'll go and wash up first. We'll feel better for it.'

Her jaw dropped. So consumed with grief, grime and blood, the stench of death had soaked into her skin. She had never considered cleaning herself up. He had.

In the darkening night he would never see how her eyes widened. They latched onto him, her pillar of strength all day. The only reason she was going to make it.

Taking her hand in his, he said, 'We just need to be very careful. If we sprain an ankle, the boats with the injured have already left.'

With all the horrors of the day switched on repeat through her head, not once did she think she would ever be able to laugh again. But she did. It wasn't loud, it wasn't uncontrollable, but it was there. Enough for Mark to stop and shine the light near her face.

'Are you okay?'

She squeezed his hand. 'Nearly.'

They made their camp close to where they had beached the previous night. No longer hungry and as clean as was possible when you wore the same clothing you had all day, Mark flattened a patch of sand using the fallen limb of a tree. Leaving a raised strip at the top, he spread his blanket first and then indicated she should lie down.

When she settled he lay down beside her, spreading the second blanket over them. 'Not exactly camping in the outback, but close.'

His hand closed over hers. No reason for it, no excuse not to.

She nudged her shoulder closer, his warmth a greedy solace she desperately wanted.

'Does that mean you live in the outback?' Her voice was only a whisper in the night, enclosing them both in their own personal space.

He rolled to his side, settling her against his chest. At the top, the raised strip of sand was the perfect pillow.

With his mouth near her ear and his strong arm wrapped around her chest, he said, 'My family owns a cattle property two hours' drive west of Chillago. Heard of it?'

'Not really. What state are we in?'

'Queensland. Inland from Cairns.'

She snuggled closer, the shock of the past twenty-four hours dimming just a fraction. 'Well, at least we're in the same state. I'm a primary school teacher doing my first year out at Kingaroy.'

Chuckling, he said, 'Peanut country.'

She giggled. 'That was the first thing I learnt about Kingaroy, too. Coming from Brisbane, that was all anyone could tell me about the place.' She could feel his smile against her neck. She liked it when his arm tightened around her.

They lay quietly for a few moments, fatigue creeping up over her body against her will. She gave a little jolt when he spoke, evidence she might have momentarily nodded off to sleep.

'I think we should enjoy the star-studded spectacle above us.' It was a moonless night and you could be forgiven for forgetting the carnage this beach had witnessed that day. 'Because any minute now I'm going to fall asleep.'

She smiled again, gripping his hand tighter.

That was her last recollection before sleep swiftly took over.

~ * ~

The morning rushed at them with a bombardment of noise. Someone on a megaphone advised all the uninjured to make their way to the beach. Women, children and couples would leave first. They spoke in a few languages, English repeated three times.

Mark gathered the blankets as shyness overcame her in the new light of day. 'Let's get you on the first boat.' Taking hold of her hand, he steered her towards the crowd gathering on the beach. Everyone was eager to be the first to get away.

Standing together, her leg no longer hurting, they watched the motorised boats do a quick job of moving the passengers to the larger waiting boats. When only a few passengers remained ahead of her, she turned to face Mark. Tears welled in her eyes, unfathomable that she should want to stay a moment longer in this place. 'Thank you so much, Mark. I would never have made it without you.'

He swallowed, his Adam's apple moving in sync with how fast her heart was beating. Tugging on her hand, he pulled her closer to his chest and lowered his face. Lightness transcended her body when his lips touched hers. Reminded of the water falling into her mouth at the little Eden they had discovered, his kiss was just as life sustaining. Not wanting it to end, she pressed closer, wrapping her arms around his waist. She barely registered when someone shuffled around her, taking her place in the queue. Like a desert flower blossoming after many seasons of no rain, his kiss was what she needed to face the news, good or bad, that awaited her at the other end.

When he released her, his grip tightened on her arm. Tears glistened around his eyes. 'You'd better go. I'll find you, Abby. I promise.'

She turned, taking the last seat on the boat before it departed.

Too late, she realised her good luck rock was still in the pocket of his shorts.

~ * ~

Six Months Later

Abby locked the classroom door for the weekend and wrapped her jacket closer to her slim chest. Tucking a scarf around her neck, she loosely knotted it and picked up her handbag. Winter was making a show.

Making her way to the car park, she waved to the other teachers leaving and wished them a great weekend. Their greetings in return washed over her.

She was good at hiding her pain.

'Abby?'

She stopped, confused. He appeared like an apparition when she recognised the voice. He was ridiculously good-looking in worn denim jeans and a white tee stretched across his broad chest. No jacket, but a brown Akubra swinging lightly in his right hand. She had never expected to see him again. Her grief so deep, she could never have gone searching for him. Not once did she expect him to keep his promise. How could she hold him to it? Sorrow had a way of digging you deeper into your own misery. For her, only a shell remained: brittle, fragile and ready to crack at any moment.

Her voice came out barely a whisper. 'Mark.'

With a few strides he was there, his Akubra forgotten, dropping to the ground. 'Abby.' His liquid brown eyes delved into hers and learnt all there was to learn. 'You never found them, did you?'

Tears easily trickled down her face. They did most days. 'We never found my sister. Zoe survived.'

'Aw … Abby, come here.'

His strong arms wrapped protectively around her with a good, strong hug. The type she badly needed. When he stepped back, he said, 'I've got something for you. I hope it cheers you up.'

Surprising herself, she smiled. But then he had been able to make her laugh at a time when it seemed improbable it could ever happen again.

He drew out a jewellery case and rubbed the burgundy velvet outer with his thumb.

'Remember those black rocks we found?'

She nodded. She remembered everything of those days. Her head refused to let a single thing slip out.

'Well, my Grandad was ecstatic. He couldn't believe I had picked up genuine black onyx *and* from Brazil. He went on for a day telling me how it was formed in the gas cavities of lava and supposed to have all sorts of mystical powers.'

She smiled at his infectious tone.

'So I asked him if he could make me a pendant. In an instant he had a group of his lapidary mates around, their sole purpose to create this for you.'

Her face jerked up, lost for a moment in his sincere gaze. When he flipped the case open, her eyes followed his strong, sinewy fingers lifting the necklace out. He leaned in closer, giving her the chance to inhale everything about him; earth, sun, man *and* life.

Loosening and then completely removing her scarf, he said, 'The onyx has to be touching your skin.' He did up the clasp and stuffed the scarf in his jeans pocket.

'Why's that?'

With his fingers resting lightly on her neck, warmth spread, thawing ice that for too long had set in.

His gaze never wavered from hers. 'There are many mystical theories about onyx, but one of them is that it helps release sorrow and grief, bringing you good fortune and personal strength.' A beat of silence followed. Her breath caught in her throat. 'I lost one of my mates, too.'

'Oh, Mark.' Wrapping her arms around his neck, she could feel the onyx connecting them. With tears cascading down her cheeks and in a muffled voice, she asked, 'And you believe all this?'

His hold tightened. 'Right now I want to believe anything.'

She fought to loosen the hold grief had over her. Yes, her tears were tinged with a lot of sadness, but they also carried something new.

Hope.

The Most Precious Jewel
By
Courtney Clark Michaels

There was a policeman in her shop.

The finely tuned survival instincts of a career criminal's daughter stopped Mae Warner in her tracks. A burning tingle of awareness, of the wariness drummed into her by her father, trickled down her spine as she assessed the situation.

Male. Over six feet. Dark hair. Tanned skin. Suit. A detective. His back was to her, revealing a bulge under the fine wool tailoring. Physically fit. Ignoring the display cases.

It was the last part that worried Mae. As the owner of a jewellery boutique in the trendy Melbourne suburb of St Kilda, she sold her designs to customers from all walks of life. Cops—like everyone else—got married, celebrated births, anniversaries, Christmas. Mae had sold numerous pieces to members of Australia's finest, but this particular public servant didn't seem like he could care less about the glittering jewels that sparkled up at him from their soft grey velvet displays.

Then he turned, and the apprehension tightening Mae's chest ballooned into a ball of fear that bounced from her heart to her stomach and back again.

His dark eyes bored into hers, a heady mix of chocolate and sin, designed to ruin her. Mae's abdomen clenched as her eyes travelled down from the deadly temptation of his long-lashed eyes, past a perfect nose to full, luscious lips.

'Lucio Roselli.'

The name fell from Mae's lips unconsciously, lingering in the air between them as her blood pounded through her system, her pulse fluttering at her wrist like a swarm of butterflies having a collective seizure.

Lucio smiled, revealing a set of perfect white teeth.

'Mae Belle Ellis.'

His use of her former surname was enough to shake Mae to her senses.

'It's Mae Warner now.'

'Are you married?' His voice, as smooth as silk and as light as a feather, slid over her, the rich timbre combined with the potency of his question prickling her skin. A shiver ran through her, which she tried desperately to hide by moving around the case to her left and approaching him from behind a barrier of glass and precious stones.

'No. What can I help you with, Lucio?'

'It's Luke now,' the Italian god countered, echoing her earlier statement. 'I'm here about onyx.'

Relief swelled in Mae like a tidal wave. No questions. No accusations. Just jewellery. The pounding of her heart, which had been battling the dulcet tones of Adele over the store speakers for aural supremacy, quelled as Mae felt her composure return.

'Onyx. Fabulous. I have some cufflinks and a series of onyx rings. Or there is a stunning tie pin in the estate section, left to the store by the family of a lovely local gentleman.'

Lucio—*Luke*—shook his head.

'Sorry, Mae. I should have been clear. I'm here about stolen onyx.'

~ * ~

Luke watched in fascination as Mae's spine noticeably stiffened. She drew herself up to her full height, her eyes flashing emerald fire at him.

Those eyes.

He would have gladly burned in their blaze back when they were teenagers growing up in the Italian-Australian suburb of Carlton. Even now, heat coursed through his system as she stared him down, her creamy skin flushed as her gorgeous mouth compressed.

'This is a legitimate business, *Lucio*,' she snapped,

emphasising his given name in a way that took him straight back to Carlton and the scores of women who had uttered it in the very tone of displeasure Mae used now. His mother. His nonna. Aunties, teachers, girlfriends.

He held up his hands in surrender.

'I know, I know. It's for work. I'm a detective.'

'I'm aware.'

A spurt of pleasure softened his mouth into a grin. She knew?

'You followed my career?'

'I followed the presence of a man wearing a six-hundred-dollar merino suit and a concealed firearm in a shoulder holster in my shop to its logical conclusion.'

Damn.

She might be the daughter of the infamous Louis Ellis, but the fact that she'd made him so quickly in plainclothes stung.

'A piece has gone missing recently in a burglary. A Roman onyx cameo, circa first century A.D. The Augustan period, I believe. Its value is estimated at around forty thousand dollars.'

Luke removed the paperwork on the stolen jewellery from his pants pocket and handed it across the counter to Mae. She took it hesitantly and unfolded the documentation, her eyes flicking quickly over the insurance appraisal.

Luke waited until she had finished, until her gleaming green eyes lifted to his again.

'I need to speak to Louis.'

Ice in his veins couldn't have frozen Luke more than the scorn on her face as she registered his words. She dropped the paperwork on the glass in front of him and stepped backwards, as though the delicate silver chains behind her could ward him off any better than the contempt in her voice.

'Daddy worked exclusively in the art business. *Worked* being the operative word.'

'It's not that, Mae Belle. I need his help.'

~ * ~

Lucio Roselli.

His name had been swirling around in Mae's head for the last three days. Ever since he left her shop with nothing but her latest catalogue and a promise that she would ask her father to meet with him. She could still feel his hot eyes on her at work when she sat in the back room of the store, dropping a Kashmir sapphire into an art deco setting; in the evenings when she cuddled up with her cat, Maurice, to watch the cooking channel. At night, when she showered and slipped between her cool Egyptian cotton sheets, the air conditioning on to combat the sticky heat of Melbourne's March weather. And more than anything, she could hear the rich tone of his voice, asking the fateful question.

'Are you married?'

Some detective he was if he couldn't deduce that a former thief's daughter might be better off using her mother's maiden name when starting up a jewellery business. But more than that, it was her response to the question in the days since he'd asked that bothered her.

She did want to be married. Although not Italian by birth, her upbringing in Carlton had left her longing for rowdy family dinners around long wooden tables, for celebrations and festivities with children of her own. And Luke's sudden reappearance in her life had reminded her of a time when she'd naively thought he might be the boy she'd like to marry. When he used to linger over cannoli at the bakery where she worked on Lygon Street and help her clean up when she worked the late shift. When he bought her a coffee and a pink rose at the Christmas market. When he'd asked her to see a movie with him on her sixteenth birthday.

She could still see the hope in his kind, dark eyes, his skin tanned from the summer sun, a football under one arm, his blue T-shirt stretched across the chest of a man that belonged to a boy. But she was the only child of a working criminal and there was one rule her father had drummed into her for as long as she could remember.

Don't attract attention.

As much as she had adored Lucio Roselli, he was renowned for replacing his girlfriends on an almost monthly cycle. Dating a known Lothario in Little Italy would have attracted more attention for that month than Mae had received in a lifetime. She'd turned him down, hating her father for his career in that moment more than ever. And Lucio Roselli had never tried for a cannoli, a coffee or a chance with her again.

Now, ten years on, she sat by the window of a St Kilda cafe watching a skinhead in a tulle skirt performing skateboard tricks with his collie on the street outside while her teenage crush and her ex-con father discussed stolen jewels and the Melbourne fence market three tables across from her over macchiatos.

Louis's bark of a laugh cut across the ambient cafe noise and soft reggae-style music, drawing Mae's attention. Turning away from the skateboarder outside, pleasure raced down her spine as she saw her father and Luke standing to shake hands.

Of all the cops and all the burglaries in the world ...

Fate might have brought Luke Roselli into her life again, but it was only temporary. As soon as he located the stolen onyx he would be gone again. And she'd be right back where she started all those years ago in Carlton—a warm memory of dark eyes to hold tight to her heart as she drifted off to sleep. Nothing more.

~ * ~

The heady aroma of freshly baked bread and the soft spittle of a graffiti artist's aerosol can filled the air as Luke guided Mae gently past the palm trees and mishmash of shopfronts that lined Acland Street.

'Louis is a good man,' he said as they approached the colourful towers and garish clown entrance of Luna Park.

A brilliant smile lit up Mae's face, causing his gut to tighten. She'd always been pretty, but like this, in the early afternoon light, with her auburn ponytail swinging behind her and her face open, without the fine lines of worry that had been creasing her forehead since he first saw her in the store, she finally reminded him of the young girl from Carlton he'd been so enamoured with.

'He is,' she agreed, enthusiastically. 'I couldn't ask for a better father. I was so young when Mum died. But Dad made sure I always knew I was loved. He was always there for me. He still is.'

'It couldn't have been easy, with his job,' Luke replied, reaching out and catching her hand. Mae looked down at their joined hands as Luke linked his fingers through hers. Warmth flooded his arm. How soft and *right* she felt entwined with him.

Yes. Like this.

'Not easy, I suppose,' Mae acknowledged with a tilt of her head. 'But he did his best to shield me from a lot of it. He never took meetings at the house and I know he took some risks working locally after Mum died so he wouldn't have to leave me for a job. But I never knew any different. I've had a long time to think about his career choices, and although I don't agree with them, I've come to the conclusion that I would rather have a retired thief who loves and cares for me for a father than one who works legitimately but misses birthdays and dinners because he's always travelling or yelling into a cell phone or some such nonsense.'

'You don't worry he'll go back to the job now you're grown up and settled?' Luke kept his voice even despite the weight that settled in his chest at the thought. If Louis ever started working the Melbourne art scene again, chances were Luke would be the one assigned to catch him. He liked Louis, and the idea of hurting Mae by hunting her father down caused panic to flutter in his chest.

Mae's laugh floated above them on a wave of warm sea air.

'I'm sure it's a genuine concern for you, Detective Roselli,' she smiled. 'But no. He promised he was done when I finished university and Louis has never broken a promise to me in his life. Besides,' she grinned up at him conspiratorially, 'several of my friends and I have developed a terrible habit of locking ourselves out of our apartments and workplaces on a semi-regular basis. Dad likes to feel needed.'

Admiration and lust bubbled through Luke as he looked down at the smiling, open face of his boyhood crush. The tenacity and nerve in Mae that had intrigued him as a teenager had matured as she'd aged. A sudden, desperate need to wrap her up in his arms and worship the gritty, witty beauty she had become roared to life inside Luke, humming through his bloodstream as they approached the address Mae had given him.

'I should have tried harder for you, Mae Belle.'

Mae's green eyes widened at his words, then quickly dropped towards their joined hands.

'It wouldn't have done any good,' she murmured. 'I couldn't have dated anyone then. Not with Dad working. It was so important that we keep under the radar.'

'What about now?' Luke persisted, urged on by the whisper of regret he heard in her tone.

'You're a cop, Luke,' Mae reminded him. 'Dating Louis Ellis's daughter isn't going to be a good look for you with the force.'

'It doesn't matter.' The words tumbled out of his mouth on a tide of desire as he turned to face her on the tree-lined street.

'I want you, Mae Belle. I've always wanted you.'

The warm sun beat down on his neck as he bent his mouth towards hers. Her honeyed breath slid across his cheek as he brushed his lips lightly across hers, twice, three times. Adrenaline fizzed in Luke's chest as he deepened the kiss, revelling in the way Mae's mouth opened to him, in the sweet taste of her.

Luke dipped his head and dropped a kiss on Mae's throat, just under her ear. The thrumming of her pulse beat a tango against his lips, dizzying in its sensual promise. A groan tore from his throat as he lost himself in the bright white heat of attraction that arced between them.

'Get a room! '

The cry from a passing car washed over Luke like a cold shower as he stepped back from Mae's warmth, short of breath and most definitely big on ideas. Like trying that again. Horizontally.

'Mae—'

'We can't do this.' She cut him off. 'I'm sorry.'

Luke stared in amazement as she darted up the nearby steps to her apartment complex and keyed in the code with record speed, slipping through the gate before he could find something—anything—to say to stop her.

~ * ~

'You've been staring at that ring a while now, honey.'

The rough burr of Louis's voice wrapped around Mae like a blanket, a comfort she craved after a long week of sleepless nights. Looking up, she saw her father slumped against the arch that separated the store from her private workshop.

'I didn't hear you come in.'

'That's the point.' Her father stepped forward to kiss her on the cheek. 'You're not looking too sharp, ace.'

He lifted the glass cleaner and a chamois cloth from beside the register and began polishing the display case.

Mae sighed, and bent down to place the ruby and diamond ring back onto its prominent stand in the coloured gems section.

'Have you heard about the onyx piece Luke asked you to look into?'

'I did.' Louis eyed her carefully.

Heat rolled over Mae's cheeks and she looked down, arranging a stand or two and silently cursing the fair skin that gave her away when she was embarrassed.

'The deal's happening today. I told Lucio what I knew. I think they're going to try for a buy-bust situation at the fence's.' Her father's voice was quiet. 'He's a good man, Mae. He cares about you. He always has. I can see it in his eyes. He looks at you the way I used to look at your mother.'

Mae's head shot up at her father's final statement, pinning her father's direct green gaze with her own.

'The life I chose wasn't easy on you, Mae. I know that and I'm sorry for it. I saw the way you two felt about each other growing up. But you and Lucio are adults now. There's nothing holding you back if you want to be together.'

The hot prickle of tears bit at the back of Mae's eyes.

'But—his job, your past. What if I cause him trouble in his career?'

Louis smiled serenely.

'L'amore vince sempre.'

Love conquers all.

~ * ~

Luke shifted uncomfortably as the final stitch pulled through the flesh of his upper left arm.

'Good thing it's not your paperwork arm,' the nurse joked, finishing off the tie.

'Hilarious,' Luke replied dryly. Obviously comedic talent

wasn't necessary to work in The Royal Melbourne Hospital's ER.

The other man laughed as he began tidying up his equipment.

'You'll be right, mate. Plenty of pretty girls willing to nurse a man back to health.'

'He doesn't need any other girls.' Mae's voice rang clearly through the curtained cubicle.

Luke's head spun from a combination of blood loss and speed as he swung to face the opening of the privacy curtain.

'Why are you here?' Shock sharpened his words.

'Why are you hurt?' Mae countered. She lowered herself to a sitting position on the bed, examining his wound site. 'I called your station and they said I could find you here.'

'But why?'

Mae smiled, and hope flared in Luke like a beam of light.

'Because I want you, Lucio Roselli. I've always wanted you. I've been scared over the years, first that dating you would cause my father problems and then, when I saw you again, that I'd cause you problems. But I want to take a chance on you.'

'*Grazie a Dio.*' Luke exhaled, leaning forward to capture her lips in a warm kiss. 'Finally.'

He was barely aware of the nurse slipping out of the cubicle as Mae cradled his injured arm against her chest.

'You were shot?'

'Just a little bit. The bullet grazed me. And hey'—Lucio leaned back to dig in his pants pocket—'I found the onyx.'

Mae examined the piece carefully, her auburn hair falling over one shoulder as she admired the cameo.

'It's stunning.' Her voice was reverential.

Luke placed his arm carefully around Mae's back, cradling her to him after a lifetime of dreams, and peppered her forehead with kisses.

'It's beautiful. But I'm holding the most precious jewel in this room. And I'm never letting her go.'

What Mari Found
By
Shannon McEwan

There's a moment in Whitby,
when the weather's just right,
that treasure can be found on the shore—
—if you know what you're looking for.

Yorkshire, 1877

Before she even got out of bed, Mari could hear the change of wind in the distant crash of the surf and the cries of the seabirds. Sure enough, when she padded over to her bedroom window, she could just make out, in the pre-dawn sky, clouds scudding west over Whitby rooftops. With the tide on its way out the shore would soon be covered with thick weed that hid ... who knew what? Maybe something precious. Maybe something rare. Mari scrabbled for her stockings and boots. If she was quick she'd get half an hour down on the beach before she needed to head back to start work at the millinery shop.

Downstairs, Ma had left breakfast ready on the kitchen table. It was the work of a moment for Mari to gulp down a mug of strong tea, pull a thick shawl about her shoulders and swipe up a dripping-butty on her way to the door. She took a quick bite as she stepped out onto the cold, cobbled street, and then swung around—straight into Ma.

'Mari!'

Mari quickly swallowed her half-chewed mouthful. 'Sorry, Ma.'

Ma raised her eyebrows and then, because she was Ma,

reached out dry, worn fingers to pull the shawl over Mari's head. Mari put up with the fussing in silence. It didn't matter that she was twenty years old—if she gave cheek, she'd be stuck on the street until she was due at the shop.

'You're off to the shore then,' said Ma.

That much was obvious.

Ma tucked the ends of the shawl around Mari's waist. 'I expect your beach friend'll be there already.'

'I expect he will,' said Mari, because of course Ant would be there on a morning like this, looking for washed-up amber and jet to make into jewellery for his uncle's shop.

Mari waited to be sent off with a sharp 'make sure you wash up proper afore work,' but instead Ma reached out and took Mari's free hand firmly between her own. A queer look came over her face.

'You know, Luv,' she said, queerer still, 'you won't always be able to go off down the beach like this—with young Antony Branco, I mean. Some people might not understand.'

'What's to understand? There's no wrong in walking on the beach and looking for jet and the like.' But she knew that Ma wasn't talking about right and wrong, but about town busybodies sticking their noses where they oughtn't.

Ma pursed her lips and squeezed Mari's hand a little tighter. 'I've just been speaking with old Mr Holloway. He says the *Rishanglys* 'll dock today.'

Which meant that Edward Grimley, the new master of the steamship *Rishanglys*, would be in town by the morrow.

Mari waited for her heart to dance. Wasn't that what was meant to happen when you thought of seeing a man who'd all but said he'd be courting you as soon as he'd set himself up in the world? But all she felt was twitchy. Keen to make the most of her time with Ant. Keen to get going before it was too late.

'We should fix your hair tonight,' Ma said, suddenly all businesslike as she let go of Mari's hand. 'Don't spend too long at the beach—and make sure you wash up proper afore work.'

Down on the shore, a group of fisherwomen were collecting driftwood. Mari greeted them on her way to where Ant was turning over briny weed with a stick. His thick blue-black hair was wild from the spring sea gale, because—as usual—he wasn't wearing a cap. He wore his hair longer than other Whitby lads. Maybe it was on account of him having an Italian father, or maybe it was because he'd lived all over before coming to Whitby six years ago to prentice to his uncle, but Ant was different in other ways, too. Different in the way he moved and different in the way he thought about things. Any more different and he'd run into trouble for sure. Still, most people seemed to like his easy manners. Mari just liked that Ant seemed to enjoy being her friend as much as she enjoyed being his.

He looked up as she walked towards him, his lean, olive skinned face breaking into a broad grin. 'Finally managed to get out of bed then, did you?'

She grinned back. 'Much luck?'

Ant made a rude sound and dug into the canvas satchel over his shoulder, pulling out two small, grey fossil fragments. 'Nothing but these. No use to anyone I reckon, not even the folk at the museum.' He shrugged. 'I was just about to go back up to the shop.' He thrust the fossils back into his satchel, then reached inside his coat. 'Course, now that you're here, I might as well give you this.' His voice was over-casual in a way that made Mari's breath quicken. 'Close your eyes.'

Mari shut her eyes tightly. Even knowing that the surprise was likely another of the beads that Ant made to practice his craft, she couldn't help but do a little jig of anticipation.

'You sure you want it?' he teased.

'Get on with you!'

The small object he placed in her palm was still warm from lying next to his body and when he closed her fingers over it, cradling her hand for an instant in his, her heart thumped fit to run away.

'You can open your eyes now.'

The bead was flat and round, about the size of a thick farthing. It was fashioned from some kind of black stone with a top layer of white that had been carved to reveal, in delicate shades of grey, a tiny sanderling. The bird's head was tilted just so, its feathers fluffed against the cold.

'When I was carving it, I was thinking about how much you like watching the shorebirds.'

Mari gently traced the outline of the bird with her forefinger, half expecting the feathers to feel as soft as they looked. 'When you said you'd been making cameos I thought you meant those shell brooches with ladies' heads on them. I never thought … '

'Well, I've done a few of the ladies' heads too, only they're in the onyx.'

'Onyx?'

'That's what the black stone is called.'

Mari rolled the word over her tongue. *Onyx*. She looked up. 'Could I see them some time—the ladies' heads?'

'Maybe. Depends. Uncle Ged wants to send them down to London. He thinks they'll get a better price there than they would here with the summer tourists.' Ant hesitated, as if deciding whether to say more.

'Go on.'

'Well, it might not mean anything, but the dealer that Ged's talking of, he sells to the Queen.'

The Queen! 'Ant, Her Majesty could end up wearing something you made. She might even ask you to make her something special—'

Ant waved the thought away with his hand. 'Not likely— about the Queen asking me to make something special, I mean. This dealer of Ged's is known for taking credit for other folks' work.'

'That doesn't sound right.'

'Maybe. Thing is, his brass is good, even after he takes his cut, and …' Ant looked out to sea, his face thoughtful. 'There's things I could do with a few extra pounds in my pocket.'

Mari watched him, side-on. It seemed wrong that people could wear Ant's jewellery without knowing anything about him. Still, there was no denying that money made things easier or that it gave you choices. If Edward Grimley's family hadn't been so decent after Pa died on one of their ships—if they hadn't made sure that Mari and Ma could get by comfortably—life would have been much harder over the last few years.

'That steamer out there,' Ant said suddenly, jutting his chin towards the horizon. 'Any idea which it is?'

Mari wasn't as good at recognising ships as most folk in town, but she knew this ship. She would have wagered anything that Ant knew it, too. 'The *Rishanglys*,' she said, her gut tightening. 'Mr Holloway says she'll dock today.'

'So you'll be seeing Edward Grimley then?'

Mari nodded, unhappy at Ant's change in mood. 'I guess.'

Ant gave her a half-smile that wasn't quite right. 'It's time I got going. I'll be seeing you.' Then he was off, striding away like he couldn't bear to spend one minute more on the beach.

~ * ~

All day, all anyone said to Mari was how glad she must be to see the *Rishanglys* coming back safe to port, and how she'd no doubt be making herself extra pretty next day in case *anyone in particular* should come a-calling. And all the while, Ant's onyx bead burned away at the bottom of her skirt pocket.

That evening, Ma didn't say a thing about Edward Grimley, but as soon as they'd washed up the tea things, she set to wrapping Mari's hair into big, fat rag-curls. Later, she shooed Mari upstairs early. 'Get a good night's sleep, Luv,' she said. 'You'll need to look your best tomorrow.'

Mari wondered what would happen if she didn't 'look her best' the next day. Would Edward Grimley decide, against the expectations of all of Whitby, that he wouldn't court her after all?

Before getting into bed, she slid the onyx bead onto the twisted linen thread that held all the other beads that Ant had given her over the years.

Jet, amber, fossil, agate, jasper.

Ant had given her the first one on the day he found her crying on the shore. It was after Edward's father, Mr Grimley, had come with the news that Pa had been killed at sea. Had Edward been with Mr Grimley on that visit? Maybe. It was hard to remember. Her memory of Ant that day, though, was alive like the bird on the onyx bead. It had been the day they'd first met properly. He'd sat next to her on the beach until she had no more tears left to cry, and then pulled from his pocket a handful of jet beads he'd made for practice, inviting her to choose one as a gift. *It's not much*, he'd said, *but it will help you remember that I'm thinking of you.*

Even when he was sixteen years old, Ant had been different.

Since then, Ant had given her twenty beads all told. Looking at them now, strung together in a mismatched necklace, Mari could see, plain as night and day, the story of how Ant's skill grown, along with their friendship. Surely nothing could take that away from her? Her gut clenched, just as it had on the beach. She clutched the beads tightly. Then she slipped them under her pillow and doused the lamp.

~ * ~

At exactly three pm the next day, Edward arrived at the front door, ship-shape-and-Whitby-fashion in his master's uniform, looking uneasy in that way born seamen do when forced to walk on dry land. Ma ushered him in with an innocent, 'Well, ain't this a nice surprise,' as if it were commonplace for her and Mari to sit around downstairs, done up to the nines, doing nothing in particular. He was barely through the door, though, before Ma slipped away upstairs 'to get something,' leaving him and Mari alone together.

After a moment's confusion, Mari remembered her manners and offered him tea with a thick slice of fruit brack. Edward wolfed down the brack but refused a second slice, the colour rising in his already ruddy face.

'Nah Mari, the cake be right, but there's sommit I want to talk to you about.' He paused.

Maybe he's not sure about this either, thought Mari. *Maybe we don't have to do what everyone expects ...*

And then he placed a small leather-covered box onto the table.

'Edward—'

'Open it.'

She had expected that Edward, when he visited, would invite her to walk out with him. She hadn't expected that Edward Grimley, staunch and predictable, would skip the courting and, without any proper talk of prospects or intentions, go straight to giving her a betrothal token. 'I don't—'

He slid the box closer to her. 'It's not what you think. Open the box, and then we'll talk.'

It's not what you think ...

Mari was the one who did all the really fine work at the

milliners, but her fingers fumbled as she tried to unfasten the box clasp.

When she finally got the lid open, she gasped. There, nestled against white satin, was a cameo brooch—a lady's head carved in black onyx. Every detail—from the delicate fairy flax that crowned the lady's softly curling hair, to the way the lady's skin glowed—all of it was carved with a familiar touch. A loving touch.

'The lady on the brooch ... you see who it is, don't you?' said Edward.

Mari swallowed, 'Aye, I see.'

Edward nodded. 'When I went into Ged's shop yesterday, I only meant to get an idea of what was there.' He shrugged. 'Anyway, Ged said he thought I should look at some of the cameos his nephew had made. There were about ten all up. Some were in shell, some were in this black stone.' He looked her in the eye. 'But every single one of them looked like you.'

'Edward, I—'

'Hear me out, Mari. I know that when these artist types fix on one woman there's usually no harm in it, that's it's just about the work—and Antony Branco is an artist for sure. I bought this brooch,' he gestured to the box on the table, 'because it's as fine a piece as I've ever seen. But then when I was leaving the shop, Branco himself walked in. The way he looked at me ... Well, suffice to say, I don't think he carves your likeness over and over just because you have a pretty face.'

Mari sat with her hands clasped in front of her, staring at the cameo.

'You didn't know, did you?' he said.

She shook her head. No, she hadn't known, even though the truth had been plain in every bead Ant had ever given her.

After a long silence, Edward said, 'I'm going to ask you a question Mari, and I want you to answer straight for both our sakes—should I court you, or no?'

It was like seeing the sun after living for months in fog and Mari suddenly found herself liking Edward more than she ever had. 'I think,' she said carefully, 'that you're a good friend to me, but that there are lasses in town who would make you a much better wife.'

Edward nodded. 'My thanks to you for speaking so plain.' He gestured to the cameo. 'If you'd like the brooch, it's yours, though I'll understand if you'd rather not take such a gift from me.'

Mari thought of how Ant had been content to let the cameos go to London without a backwards glance. And then she thought of the beads on her friendship necklace, most of them carved just for her.

She reached out, closed the cameo box, and handed it back to Edward.

Ma, of course, had been standing half way up the stairs the whole time, listening to every word. When Edward left she came back down and pulled Mari close. 'Are you sure this is what you want, Luv?'

'Yes. Yes, it is. Do you mind?'

Ma smiled. 'Antony Branco's a good lad. He'll never make as much brass as a ship's master, but he works hard.' She kissed Mari on the cheek. 'And he makes you happy. That's all I need to know.'

~ * ~

Next morning, Mari was off to the beach before dawn, her string of beads heavy in her skirt pocket.

Ant was on the shore already, his dark hair wilder than usual. He looked tired in the pale-grey light, and when he greeted her it was without his usual warmth.

Mari cleared her throat. 'I saw Edward Grimley yesterday.' She clutched at the beads through the fabric of her skirt, drawing on them for courage. 'He showed me a cameo he'd bought—one of the ones you made.' She swallowed hard. 'Ged's right. The others should sell well in London.'

Ant's eyes narrowed as if he didn't quite trust what she was saying, which was fair enough given she was making a mess of it all.

'So you liked it then,' he said. 'The cameo?'

'Yes, I liked it very much. Although ... I wouldn't like to wear it.'

Now she had his full attention. 'And why would that be?'

Mari took a deep breath 'A brooch like that is meant for someone with different tastes. A captain's wife maybe, who wants the town to know her consequence.'

Ant went still. 'So what's to your taste then?'

Mari pulled out the string of beads and offered it to him, cupped in both hands. 'This,' she said simply.

Ant's mouth stretched slowly into the wide grin that Mari loved so much. 'May I?' he asked.

She nodded, her mouth too dry to speak.

Ant took the string of beads and wrapped it around her wrist. Once. Twice. Then he carefully tied the ends, and threaded his fingers through hers, drawing her to him for a single kiss on the lips. It was soft and it was sweet and it tasted of the sea.

When he pulled back she could hear, clear above the sound of the surf, the *whit-whit-whit* of sanderlings calling for a mate.

Ant grinned at her once more. 'Fancy a walk along the beach then?'

Mari grinned back. 'There's nothing I'd like better.'

Want to try something a little spicier?

Why not try our Spicy Bites Anthology?

Spicy Bites 2017

Tattoo

http://romanceaustralia.com/shop/

Little Gems 2018

The gem for the 2018 Little Gems anthology will be…

Jade

For details of how to submit a story, please see Romance Writers of Australia's website
http://romanceaustralia.com/contests/aspiring-contests/little-gems/

Previous Little Gems anthologies can be purchased from the Romance Writers of Australia store
http://romanceaustralia.com/shop/

About the Authors

Heidi Catherine

Heidi Catherine is a Melbourne-based writer. This is the fourth consecutive year she's been fortunate enough to have a story published in Little Gems. Other career highlights include winning Romance Writers of Australia's inaugural Emerald Pro award for her young adult novel, The Soulweaver. Heidi was a highly commended author in The Hope Prize, judged by Kate Grenville, Cate Blanchett and Quentin Bryce. As a result, her story, The Extra Piece, was published by Simon & Schuster in a collection of the winning entries. Please visit www.heidicatherine.com to learn more, or say hello on Facebook or Twitter.

Courtney Clark Michaels

Courtney Clark Michaels has been reading and writing romance since she first pilfered a novel out of her mother's bedroom at the tender age of thirteen. While her new writing hobby didn't endear her to teachers, it did make maths more interesting for her friends. Her passion for writing strong, independent heroines and sexy, smart men is equal only to her passions for travel, online shopping and patting other people's dogs. Courtney is lucky enough to live in the heart of the New Zealand wine-making region with her own alpha man, her gorgeous stepdaughter and a hyperactive poochon named Kevin.

Kat Colmer

Kat Colmer is a Sydney-based Young and New Adult author who writes coming-of-age stories with humour and heart. The recipient of several writing awards, she has won the Romance Writers of Australia First Kiss contest as well as the Romance Writers of America On the Far Side contest.

Kat has a Master of Education in Teacher Librarianship and loves working with teens and young adults. Her debut Young Adult romance The Third Kiss is now available from all good online book retailers. Find out more at www.katcolmer.com or connect on Twitter, Instagram and Facebook.

Frances Dall'Alba

Seven years ago Frances began to nurture her passion for writing. Becoming a member of Australia's RWA was an important turning point in this journey.

Juggling a family business and raising three teenage daughters, left minimal time to devote to writing. What time she could spare she guarded fiercely. Not fazed by hard work there is nothing more satisfying than watching her word count increase as a new and exciting story evolves. She was a finalist in RWA's 2016 Emerald Award.

Frances lives in tropical Far North Queensland where the conditions for writing are perfect. Find her at her blog: www.francesdallalba.blogspot.com.au

Imelda Evans

Imelda is an Australian writer who likes books, baths and baking, coffee, cocktails and craft, family, friends and food… and a good lie in the hammock when the alliteration fails her!

Humoured by a supportive husband and daughter, she writes novels about women's lives – the dramas, the challenges, the joys and the occasional loaded gun – and how they get through them with a sense of humour and a little help from their friends.

This is her first appearance in Little Gems but she hopes not her last!

If you want to know more, you can find her at **www.imeldaevans.wordpress.com**.

Fiona Greene

Fiona Greene loves romance – reading it, and now writing it. Her works range from contemporary stories with strong heroines and even stronger heroes, to journeys across time and space, exploring the infinite possibilities of romance across the universe. Fiona's motto: What's not to love about a futuristic military leader with a spacecraft? Unless it's a sexy farmer with a Ute?

Fiona lives in Brisbane, Australia, with her husband and two incredibly spoilt dogs. You can find her online at http://www.fionagreene.weebly.com

Jillian Jones

Jillian Jones is a writer and certified life coach residing on the beautiful Sunshine Coast, Queensland with her incredibly supportive husband, two creative children and a demanding Devon Rex cat. She loves to explore new age elements, healing modalities and sometimes a touch of magical realism within the contemporary romance genre. Along with affirming the notion that love heals and love transforms; expect to encounter crystals, angels, clairvoyants, and the occasional portal when reading her stories. She holds a Bachelor of Arts from the University of Queensland majoring in English and Art History. Explore more at: www.jillianjones.com

Jeff Kenneally

Jeff Kenneally has always written, but mostly non-fiction in relation to his long career as an Intensive Care Paramedic. Anyone who knows Jeff knows him as a true story teller. He writes a regular blog in which he recalls the human side of cases he has attended over the years, written with empathy and compassion. When Jeff spins a yarn he quickly draws a crowd. His motto is 'never let the truth get in the way of a good story'.

His next venture is to focus on fiction – this short story was his first dabble and he is hooked.

Caitlyn Lynch

Caitlyn Lynch is an Australian mother of two who has always enjoyed reading and writing romantic fiction. Happily married to her very own tall, dark and handsome for 14 years and counting, she draws on a rich imagination to create new scenarios for her steamy contemporary romances.

She has lately started Shenanigans Press, dedicated to helping first-time authors gain experience in the world of self-publishing through a series of short story anthologies.

You can find her at her website caitlynlynch.com, or on Facebook, Twitter and Tumblr.

Fiona Marsden

As a child, Fiona preferred to play with Barbie dolls rather than baby dolls so she could create a cast of characters and force them to live out her fantasies. Which all came into focus when she learned how to read, and write.

Marriage and a family distracted her for a while, but she did keep reading. She's heavily involved in a local disability focussed organisation.

Now she writes contemporary and historical romances with an occasional dabble into sci-fi/fantasy. She has a novella published in an indie anthology called Beautiful Disaster and this is her second appearance in Little Gems.

Shannon McEwan

Shannon McEwan's first exposure to genre romance was via the serialised M&B novels in her Nanna's English Woman's Weekly magazines. Her Nanna had no time for That Kind of Rubbish (she only subscribed for the knitting patterns) but Shannon was hooked.

Years later, inspired by a housemate who read Georgette Heyer in the bathtub, Shannon started writing historical romance. Some of her stories have been sweet, some of them sultry. She's pretty sure her Nanna wouldn't approve of any of them.

Shannon lives, parents and writes in Melbourne's Northern suburbs. You can find her online at www.shannonmcewan.com

Jane Newton

Jane Newton is an editor who loves helping authors polish their fiction manuscripts. Occasionally she scribbles stories of her own. Keepsakes is the first romantic fiction short story she has sent out into the world and she's thrilled it has found a home in this anthology.

Rosemary Pearse

Words and music have been a driving force throughout Rosemary's life. Always a voracious reader and an occasional book seller, she squandered her youth playing in bands, writing songs and music for film, but the fuse to write fiction wasn't lit until she became a foster carer and a home-based creative outlet was needed, stat. Rosemary writes contemporary fiction and is currently working on two novels and blogs occasionally at www.writerosiewrite.wordpress.com. Blind Date is her first short story.

Stella Quinn

Stella Quinn believes romance, adventure and escapism are the reasons we love to read. Her novels are sun-filled and sea-drenched; love blooms under the palm trees of far-flung islands, or in the warm waters above sunken wrecks. 'Wow', 'captured me from the first page', 'loved it', 'hot sex', 'loved the backstory', 'everything worked!' … these are some of the comments Stella has received from Romance Writers of Australia judges. You can read more about her novels Tropic Storm and Stowaway on Stella's website www.stellaquinnauthor.com

www.ingramcontent.com/pod-product-compliance
Lightning Source LLC
Chambersburg PA
CBHW050454110726
47899CB00003B/932